© Copyright 2006 Marc Lieberman.
All rights reserved. No part of this publication may be reproduced, stored in a retrieval system, or transmitted, in any form or by any means, electronic, mechanical, photocopying, recording, or otherwise, without the written prior permission of the author.

Note for Librarians: A cataloguing record for this book is available from Library and Archives Canada at www.collectionscanada.ca/amicus/index-e.html
ISBN 1-4120-8577-2

Printed in Victoria, BC, Canada. Printed on paper with minimum 30% recycled fibre.
Trafford's print shop runs on "green energy" from solar, wind and other environmentally-friendly power sources.

TRAFFORD
PUBLISHING

Offices in Canada, USA, Ireland and UK

Book sales for North America and international:
Trafford Publishing, 6E–2333 Government St.,
Victoria, BC V8T 4P4 CANADA
phone 250 383 6864 (toll-free 1 888 232 4444)
fax 250 383 6804; email to orders@trafford.com

Book sales in Europe:
Trafford Publishing (UK) Limited, 9 Park End Street, 2nd Floor
Oxford, UK OX1 1HH UNITED KINGDOM
phone 44 (0)1865 722 113 (local rate 0845 230 9601)
facsimile 44 (0)1865 722 868; info.uk@trafford.com

Order online at:
trafford.com/06-0333

10 9 8 7 6

To my father, David: Each adventure is mere prelude to life in full.

Disclaimer:

This book is a work of fiction. Names, characters, places and incidents are the product of the author's imagination or are used fictitiously. Any resemblance to actual events, locales, or persons, living or dead, is purely coincidental. On the other hand, there is some truth to many of the events described:

There seems to be a growing consensus the Roswell Incident occurred as originally reported by the government. Further, the U.S. has readily acknowledged it is close to deploying lasers designed to disable ground and air forces. The *Andrea Doria* effect is a well-documented behavior of bats, and Arabian pigeons are truly the "alarm bells" of the Bedouin. Remarkably, a few people have managed to somewhat "domesticate" bears.

On the other hand, many mysteries remain. We really don't know what happened to the Anasazi. And of course, if the Roswell Incident actually transpired, it begs the question whether additional contacts with extra-terrestrials have occurred.

Medicine Stone Lake, Leonard Island and Tuzigoot are real places, albeit not in New Mexico. There are clues there that may help resolve some of the continuing mysteries. I leave it to you to discover more.

Acknowledgments:

I am deeply indebted to noted mystery author and educator Joyce Spizer Foy, for her careful and adept editing of the initial drafts, as well as guidance on everything literary. I am also indebted to my father, David Lieberman, whose wise and politic criticism helped shape many themes.

My great friend, Phoenix lawyer, firearms expert and motorcycle enthusiast extraordinaire Michael P. Anthony provided invaluable advice about arms, ammunition and motorbikes. Additional advice on arms and tactics were provided by kindred spirits, Phoenix police sergeants Ron Snodgrass and Christel Boeck. Many thanks to Wisconsin artist Al Hedman for the wonderful cover art. And perhaps most of all, thanks to my lifelong friends, Robert Kulick and Samuel Hess, who urged me to complete this work after I had lost faith in the process.

To all the friends and family that lent their names, experiences and bits of personality to the characters in *The Translator*, I hope you enjoy the book as much as I enjoyed including you in the story.

Marc Lieberman, October, 2006

THE TRANSLATOR

Marc Lieberman

CHAPTER ONE

Santa Fe, New Mexico

It filled her with a sense of purpose, sitting at the silent board, awash with its glow of white lights, waiting for the alarm that each day signaled danger and intrigue. For three years, Mariah had sat at this post and listened for the sounds of thieves and murderers at their work. She was the first defense against them, and as her "arrest" record proved, she was pretty good at her job.

A light to her immediate right turned amber. She turned the rheostat switch below the light, which increased the pick-up level of the microphones embedded in the walls of the home where the sound tripping the alarm light had originated. The label below the amber light read "SF 263." She didn't need to reference the manual to see whose home that was.

It was hers.

The kids! They were undoubtedly asleep, Heddy having put them to bed long ago. Heddy herself should be asleep. Mariah's mind raced, as she strained to identify the sound that tripped the alarm. She listened carefully, as she had been taught to do.

Her headset screamed, "I know you're listening."

A stranger was in the house! She threw the toggle switch immediately below the amber light, automatically dispatching a Santa Fe police car to her house.

"We're taking the children," the voice continued in a terse whisper. "They'll be returned when and if you deliver him. We'll be in touch."

Mariah felt faint. She didn't recognize the voice. But worse, she understood its message.

CHAPTER TWO

Long Island, New York

Marcus took it for the most selfish of reasons. How ironic that now, after unlocking many of its mysteries, he kept it to protect others. Protect others from themselves.

It had been three lonely but exciting years, and he was anxious to see Mariah. The trick had been to contact her without arousing suspicion. Until he saw her, he would not know whether the Sign had succeeded.

There are nearly 6,000 known languages on Earth, and Dr. Marcus Aaron spoke eighty-six of them. Yet, the Sign was not part of any tongue. It had been created on a whim, and on that whim he risked everything. Marcus couldn't help thinking that sort of thing largely reflected his behavior since adolescence.

He had last drawn the Sign for his daughter decades before, at a time when his priorities consisted of paying bills and keeping schedules. Now he had just one priority -- to stay alive long enough to see her, to perhaps convince her to come with him.

They would be watching, waiting to strike. He hoped he was ready.

* * *

Santa Fe, New Mexico

This was the second time Mariah had sat in this room. Years before, when she first had been interrogated here, she had been surprised that none of the agents wore shoulder holsters, like on TV. Now nothing seemed surprising. Angry and frightened, she began to suspect that the Bureau hadn't a clue as to Brittany and Jacob's whereabouts.

"Odds are we'll find something leading us to them. I've got the entire squad on this, and the lab's beginning work on the prints and fibers as we speak."

Keenan Darstow was a "Greybeard," Bureau jargon for an especially gifted, veteran agent. Mariah's hopes had risen when she learned Darstow had been placed in charge of her case. But with each passing hour, the chances of locating Brittany and Jacob dimmed, and Darstow's well-intentioned assurances began to ring hollow.

"Think, Mariah!" pleaded Darstow. "Where could your father be? Where could he be coming from?"

"I don't know!" Mariah gestured towards a manila-colored "sweepstakes" envelope on the green metal desk that separated them. "The postmark is from New York. I nearly tossed it as junk mail before spotting the Sign."

Mariah felt bled of tears. "I should have known there would be trouble, after what happened when he first disappeared."

Her voice began to crack, and another wave of nausea hit her. "I just can't believe they'd ransom my children for him!"

Darstow put his arms around her. "We'll tap all the phones, place agents with you around the clock. When they contact you, we may be able to trace the call. And if we find Marcus first, they'll have no hand to play."

Mariah no longer listened. Instead, she ran the scenario again in her head. After receiving the Sign, she'd been elated. Finally, she'd be reunited with her father. But somehow, by sending her the Sign, her father had placed Brittany and Jacob in mortal danger. And if harm came to them, she would see him in hell.

CHAPTER THREE

Bhojpur, Nepal

Nepal is some country, Andrew mused. He watched transfixed as traffic screamed to a standstill while a line of Buddhist monks, resplendent in their saffron robes, marched diagonally across a teeming intersection. It was stifling hot in the taxi, and he couldn't wait to reach Pratmankun.

"How much longer?" Andrew asked.

"Sleep now, mister," the driver replied. "We not come there until much time."

The thought of spending a prolonged period in the taxi turned Andrew's thoughts from his destination to his bowels. "Could you pull over? I have to go to the bathroom."

The driver chuckled. "Under seat, mister. There is batroom."

At first, Andrew felt nothing. Eventually, his fingers closed upon a tin pot with a wire handle. He yanked it free.

"You expect me to go in *this*?" Andrew indignantly replied.

"All do, mister. There no shame in dat."

"Pull over. Pull over I tell you," Andrew shouted.

The driver sighed and veered over to a fruit-filled cart pulled by a llama. Andrew leapt from the taxi, signaled the driver to wait, and set off for the nearest facilities.

Of course, no one spoke English. After what seemed like hundreds of inquiries, most of which consisted of his pointing to his fat backside, he stumbled upon a public outhouse: four holes in the earth, with a bucket of tepid water in between.

Some country, Andrew thought. Not a tissue in sight. The only paper available was his bankroll of newly-exchanged rupee notes.

Three hundred rupee later, Andrew finally understood what it meant to throw money down the toilet. It might seem funny, he thought, if he hadn't just wasted a good portion of his available cash.

He steeled himself with the thought that this was the big one. This would be the scoop that'd make the big boys notice and catapult him from the tabloids to the *Times*. He was sure only he had noticed the patterns. And if he could just tie it all together, nothing could prevent him from realizing his dream.

The cab left! Damn the driver! Damn him for having paid the full fare at the outset. He was now lost, without transportation, in a strange village whose name he didn't even know.

Seeing no cars, he walked over to a young boy bridling a llama hitched to a buggy. "Take me to Pratmankun – please?"

CHAPTER FOUR

Washington, D.C.

"Need I ask?" Boyskut smirked.

"Don't bother," Dov Bar-Lev replied.

For the past four years, they had greeted each other in this fashion. Petrovich Boyskut was a former KGB major, having defected in the pre-Gorbachev days when defection meant something. Part of his "turn package" had been a house in Georgetown, near his naturalized aunt, and $500,000 cash.

After losing part of the money at a dog track the first day he was released from protective custody, Boyskut invested the remainder in his Washington deli, the "Commie Salami." The deli, situated directly across from the Hoover Building, had instantly become a popular lunch destination for Bureau personnel. Dov wasn't sure whether that was due to its provocative name or Boyskut's superb polish sausage.

Boyskut slapped a fat polish into a sesame seed bun, drowned it in sauerkraut and hot mustard, and thrust it into Dov's eager hands.

"You really should try something, anything else, Dov. Four years of sausage will send you to an early grave."

"I might as well die happy."

Dov eased himself into his favorite booth. He was the youngest ever Assistant Director of the Bureau, charged with overseeing all criminal investigations nationwide. As challenging a life as he led, his joys were few and most importantly, familiar. He needed familiar things, like Boyskut's polish sausage, to give his topsy-turvy life some stability.

Dov smiled. Ten years ago, he might have killed Boyskut while on assignment. Now Boyskut was as close to "family" as Dov had, and Boyskut's sausage was killing him.

"Darstow's on it."

Dov's attention was instantly directed from his lunch to the booth behind him. He turned his ear closer to the knotty-pine divider separating him from the man who had mentioned Keenan Darstow.

"But why Darstow? Kidnapping isn't his jurisdiction."

"Shit, who knows? Must have some security implications. All I know is that jerk is out of my hair. I pity those poor hicks in Santa Fe."

Already exercised by the mention of Darstow's name, Dov's heart pounded against his chest upon learning Darstow was involved in a kidnapping investigation. He crooked his ear closer to the divider but, at that moment, the men suddenly rose and left.

Darstow. That son of a bitch. The Bureau had many untouchables within its ranks, but Keenan Darstow, Assistant Director of Internal Security, was the most notorious. Undoubtedly, he was the most feared. Even the Director gave Darstow free rein.

What was Darstow doing on a kidnapping? A kidnapping Dov didn't even know about.

Dov's pulse raced. Absent extraordinary circumstances, Darstow could not have assumed command of a kidnapping investigation without Dov's knowledge. The White House must be involved. Or perhaps NSA or CIA.

One thing was certain, Dov thought. Demanding an explanation from the Director or Darstow himself would get him nowhere. He had been kept out of the loop for a purpose. He would discover that purpose if it was the last thing he did.

CHAPTER FIVE

Santa Fe, New Mexico

"Yeah?"

"Thomas, this is Dov."

"Dov Bar-Lev, my favorite Jewish G-man."

"Cut it out Thomas. I need your help."

"Geez Dov, I was just about to leave town."

"This is important, Thomas. I need you to run something aground for me, and I'll even pay your unbelievably outrageous fee."

Thomas laughed. "You really must be desperate. Is this Bureau business or yours, Dov?"

"For now, mine." Dov paused. "It involves Darstow."

A long silence followed.

"Okay, what's up?"

Dov related what he had learned at the deli.

"So, all you know is Darstow's handling a Santa Fe kidnapping investigation without your knowledge or authorization?"

"Yes."

Dov didn't need to explain why he hadn't confronted Darstow about the situation directly. Thomas Kuzmic was well-versed in Bureau protocol, having served seven years as a special agent assigned to the FBI's crack counter-intelligence and Hostage Rescue teams. Before joining the Bureau, Kuzmic spent six harrowing years as a Navy SEAL stationed throughout Europe and Southeast Asia. His final two years at the Bureau were spent as a liaison to covert units of the Mossad operating in southern Lebanon. It was there that Kuzmic had first met Dov, who had been investigating the kidnapping of an American tourist by Iranian-backed fundamentalists. Kuzmic was the only other Bureau agent in theater and, after enduring a few close scrapes with Hezbolah militias, they became fast friends. Their postings had kept them apart, but they made every effort to keep in touch.

After his Lebanese posting, Kuzmic quit the Bureau and set up his own detective agency in Santa Fe. Dov never asked what prompted Kuzmic to turn in his shield. But he suspected it had something to do with Keenan Darstow, whose security teams Kuzmic somehow held responsible for the death of Kuzmic's beautiful fiancé, Lisl.

Kuzmic said, "I'll see if I can find out the details of the kidnapping without alerting anyone. Any theories?"

"Several come to mind. This may be a ploy to discredit me. On the other hand, national security issues within Darstow's jurisdiction may actually be implicated; the kidnapping could either be a minor aspect of the case or merely a cover."

"Where can I reach you?"

"Call me at home in the evening every couple of days, sooner if developments warrant. Leave no message on the machine. I'll scramble all our conversations, from both ends."

"You can do that now?"

"I'm going to have to renew your subscription to *Popular Mechanics*, Thomas. We've been able to do that for nearly a year."

"Shalom, Dov."

"Watch your ass, Thomas."

CHAPTER SIX

Pratmankun, Nepal

Pratmankun, a village of 1,400 situated at the northeastern edge of Nepal, is surrounded to the north, west, and east by three 28,000 foot peaks, some of the highest in the Himalayas. Immediately north of the village, just over towering Mount Kanchenjunga lies Communist China. A sliver of India borders the village to the east.

For years, Pratmankun had served as a staging area for Tibetan rebels fighting China's brutal occupation of the Tibetan Plain. On July 16, 1996, elements of the Peoples Liberation Army's 8th Airwing launched a helicopter raid on the rebel camps just north of Pratmankun. The rebels were taken completely by surprise, having mistakenly assumed they were impervious from helicopter attack since no chopper could achieve sufficient altitude to cross the peaks separating Pratmankun from China. Rather than crossing directly from China into Nepal however, the Chinese skirted the impassable mountains by flying southeast into India and then heading due north, below radar range, into the unprotected Pratmankun Valley.

This much Andrew knew to be unchallenged fact. The rest of what had happened the day of the attack remained shrouded in mystery, and Andrew hoped he could solve it.

"Meesta Soita?"

"Sawyer, dear fellow, soy-yer. Might you be Mr. Watsairuti?"

The man nodded. "Watsairuti. Learn Engrish by Sir Eddy."

Sir Eddy was undoubtedly a reference to Edmund Hillary, the first man to have reached the summit of nearby Mount Everest. In recent years, Hillary had devoted much of his time to cleaning up the mountain of discarded climbing debris, which as a result of his exploits and those that followed him, now littered Everest's slopes.

"Can we see the injured Chinese pilot?"

"We talk soon at piot."

Andrew smiled. Not knowing what else to do, he bowed deeply. This delighted his guide, who turned and briskly strode down the steep path at the center of the village where Andrew had earlier been deposited by his young friend with the buggy. Taking a deep breath, Andrew marched after Watsairuti, his lungs still gasping from the extreme altitude. Despite his discomfort, Andrew couldn't help admiring the incredible beauty of the mountain snows wisping over the craggy Himalayas.

They walked for about an hour. Andrew was about to request he be allowed a rest when they came to a clearing split by a small stream and bounded to the east by a stone hut. Watsairuti marched to the hut and immediately entered, not bothering to knock on the weather-beaten wooden door. Panting and sweating profusely, Andrew quickly followed at his heels.

To Andrew's right sat an emaciated Asian man on a hand-hewn wooden footstool. The man's legs were swathed in dirty, bloody gauze, and his tattered military shirt bore insignia reflecting his rank as a captain in the PLA Helicopter Corps. The man drank porridge from a tin cup held to his pursed lips by a frail peasant woman dressed in dark green batik. The man stared blankly ahead, not acknowledging their presence.

Watsairuti bent down and whispered something to the man. The man smiled and clapped. He then gestured wildly in all directions with his skinny arms, muttering something Andrew could not understand.

"So, it's true he's blind?" Andrew asked.

"He no see…Rebers not krill him because he no see. Bad to krill man no see."

Andrew pulled out his notepad and sat opposite the blind pilot.

"What is his name?"

Watsairuti translated Andrew's question, and the pilot responded flatly, "Gaiyen."

Watsairuti said, "He first piot, Gaiyen."

"How was he captured?"

Watsairuti again whispered into the pilot's ear, and as the pilot spoke, translated, "He say it was blight day, no crouds. They fly near earth, so close could touch twees with foot."

The blind pilot continued to mutter, almost in a monotone.

"When near reber camp, they spread out, sight tawget, prepare to fie missile, shoot gun."

The blind man became more agitated; his voice trembled and grew higher pitched.

"He see to his right, helicopter dive into earth, no reason! He look to his lef, helicopter point to sky, then dive to earth, no reason!"

The blind man screamed. His arms flailed in front of him. Tears streamed down his inflamed cheeks.

Watsairuti's voice grew louder. "He see blight light, so light it tousan, millin time lighter than sun. Then he no can see and…he lose control of machine and… "

The pilot sobbed hysterically.

"He wake up here, can no see. He no see again."

Touched by the pilot's agony, Andrew paused. "Did any of the other Chinese soldiers survive?"

"No. All dead but this man."

Andrew bent closer to the pilot, who had collapsed into a corner of the hut, sobbing. "What caused the bright light?"

Watsairuti smiled confidently. "It is Buddha, Mr. Soita. Rebers shoot no gun. This sign that rebers in Buddha's favor."

Andrew stared into the pitiful blind man's eyes.

"Mr. Watsairuti, ask him if he knows where the light came from?"

Watsairuti translated, but seemed perplexed by the response. "He say surely it was devil…or perhap, United State?"

CHAPTER SEVEN

Santa Fe, New Mexico

Everywhere Mariah went, agents shadowed her. Darstow would have placed an agent in her bedroom if she hadn't adamantly refused his agents access to the living quarters of the house altogether. Of course, all her mail and telephone conversations were intercepted and the stress from the kidnapping was compounded by the FBI's constant surveillance.

Mariah couldn't bring herself to go to work. Instead, she had begun shutting herself up in the house, hoping that the Professor would call, thereby hastening Brittany and Jacob's return.

She'd always loved her father. Maybe that's why she'd married Henri Bourassa, her father's protégé. Henri even looked like Marcus Aaron -- tall, broad-shouldered and dark complexioned. She thought of Henri often, usually just before bed, or when Brittany and Jacob did something that would have made Henri proud.

As occurred every time her thoughts turned to Henri, she thought about the accident. She remembered that evening clearly. She had been home cooking when Keenan Darstow first appeared at her door.

"Henri is dead," he whispered. His downcast eyes avoided hers. There had been "an accident" at the base.

After Henri's badly charred body had been buried, Darstow confided that Henri died while attempting to prevent her father from taking "top secret" government property.

"Are you saying my father killed my husband?" Mariah fixed Darstow with an icy stare.

"No. Clearly he died purely by accident. Hit by a fuel truck, as I said. But he was killed while attempting to prevent your father from stealing certain…goods. Can't you tell us where your father is?"

"As I've told you from the beginning, I haven't seen Dad since the evening before Henri's death. What is it my father's accused of stealing? What is it that Henri risked his life to save?"

"Surely Henri and the Professor told you what they were working on in Magdalena?"

"Damn it, we've been over this ground fifty times! All I know is that they had been retained to translate inscriptions on an ancient Indian relic unearthed in the vicinity of Socorro. Why the air force was interested in such a project was never explained, and with two children in diapers, I didn't really care so long as Henri received a regular paycheck. Is it the relic my father supposedly took? That Henri died attempting to preserve?"

Darstow's face became impassive. "If you don't know, Mariah, I'm simply not at liberty to say. But your father's missing, and what he has taken has sorely weakened this nation's security."

With that, Darstow abruptly turned away, and Mariah had not seen him again for the past three years – until the kidnapping.

CHAPTER EIGHT

Santa Fe, New Mexico

Thomas Kuzmic hunched behind the wheel of his battered Impala convertible and waited for Darstow's car to exit the Bureau's parking garage on East Paseo de Peralta. He had been surveilling the garage for nearly three hours. If Darstow was actually heading a local kidnapping investigation, he would operate out of the Bureau's small offices in Santa Fe, and not the safe-house near Taos.

This time, Thomas hoped he might have the jump on Darstow. The bastard had killed Lisl just as sure as he had put a gun to her head.

He thought of her fragile, aquiline face, her soft lilting accent, all gone because of Darstow's conceit. He could conjure it up exactly.

He had just left her. As he reached the outskirts of town, he saw the jets streaking in low overhead. He turned, just as their laser-guided bombs blew the Rashdod Hotel into rubble. Instantly, he had veered the Rover around and careened back. By then, the entire hotel and two adjacent buildings were smoking wreckage. They never recovered her body.

Their tryst had been as secret as his work. Covert agents were not to date journalists, much less foreign correspondents. But he knew their love was genuine, and if forced to choose between Lisl and the Bureau, Lisl it would have been.

She had been at the Rashdod Hotel to interview Ali Beshawri, a senior policy advisor to Fatah, the political arm of the PLO. They thought they might as well make a holiday of it. The hotel was famous for its croissants and jam, and Thomas got a perverse kick out of staying the night in the same hotel as a senior PLO staffer. But unknown to Thomas Kuzmic, Darstow had learned from a Libyan informant that the terrorist mastermind Abu Nidal was at the hotel as well. Darstow had relentlessly pursued Nidal throughout Europe and North Africa. The man that nailed Nidal would be a hero to the West and could write his own ticket. And so Darstow had ordered the hotel leveled, thirty-two innocent people murdered, just to kill one beast. The irony was Nidal had never even visited the hotel. Later reports placed him in Tunis the moment Lisl had been incinerated.

"There's the bastard now," Thomas whispered, as Darstow and an entourage of three agents exited the Bureau's garage and headed east. After a few seconds, Thomas slipped out of his space and followed at as extreme a distance as possible. He was well aware that Darstow's driver would be looking for tails.

Traffic was light, and Thomas found his quarry leading him to a residential district near some of the newer Canyon Road galleries. Darstow's car pulled into the carport of a small adobe whose front door was painted a striking blue. Thomas drove past the building and parked about a block and a half further east. The adobe's address was 1023 Paseo Redondo.

Thomas got out of the car and walked, in a casual fashion, back toward the adobe on the opposite side of the street. He thrust his hands into his pockets and tried to look like a lost tourist. Everywhere he glanced, people were performing yard work, painting their homes, or walking pets. Though it was a weekday afternoon, the neighborhood was a virtual beehive of activity. It all seemed wrong, somehow.

Then it struck him. Everyone about was young and extremely fit. The entire block was being staked out by Darstow's agents!

He continued walking a full block west past the adobe before turning south and circling back to his car. Thank God he'd had sense to park at least a full block away. He hoped he hadn't been photographed. It would have taken less than a minute for his mug to be identified by the Bureau's computers.

1023 Paseo Redondo. What lay behind that blue door?

CHAPTER NINE

Taos, New Mexico

"Your turn."

"Christ, I'm still achin' from the last time." Melvin rubbed his shins and searched for sympathy as he gestured to his right elbow. "Little bastard nearly broke me arm with a chair leg."

"Stop griping and feed 'em, Melvin. I was you, I wouldn't let on about having the crap beat out of me by a rug rat."

Melvin shot Piter a disgusted look and lurched toward the bedroom where they were keeping Jacob. They had nicknamed the boy "Kato," after Inspector Clouseau's sidekick with a penchant for unexpected karate attacks. Apparently, Jacob had seen one too many Ninja Turtle movies and never missed an opportunity to flail his captors with a flurry of poorly-executed, but occasionally effective, kicks and punches.

"Kid, I'm coming in, and if you so much as breathe funny, I'm gonna break your goddamn leg!" With that, Melvin unlocked the door, turned the latch and kicked open the door. In his right hand he held a tray with a peanut butter sandwich and some apple juice. He kept his left hand free, anticipating trouble. Strangely, nothing happened.

After a moment, he entered the room. It was empty! He shoved the tray onto a dresser and quickly strode into the adjoining bathroom. It was empty as well. "Damn it, Kid, where'd you go?" In a panic, he looked under the bed, even under the bathroom sink. "Christ!" The room's windows were barred, and he was sure the door was locked before he opened it.

"Piter, Kato's gone. The little bastard is plumb disappeared."

Piter rushed into the room, and together they searched it top to bottom.

"You musta forgot to lock the door when you fed 'em this morning," Melvin said accusingly.

"Hell I did," Piter retorted. "I made sure the door was locked. Little bastard musta picked it."

Piter took Melvin by the lapels of his jacket. "We gotta find that little shit Mel, or we're good as dead."

Melvin tore out of the room, with Piter at his heels. They left the door ajar.

Jacob waited a full five minutes after Piter and Melvin left the house before freeing himself from the bedroom's viga and latilla ceiling, where he had hidden himself. He had to find Brittany and escape before Piter and Melvin returned.

* * *

Santa Fe, New Mexico

"I don't think I was made, but it was definitely a Level Three stakeout. All Darstow's people, not street agents."

"So, let me get this straight, Thomas. The home is owned by a Mariah Aaron Bourassa. She works as a dispatcher for Sonitrol, a local alarm company. She has two children, Brittany and Jacob, ages nine and eleven?"

"That's the best I could hunt up on short notice, Dov. Her credit report is nothing special, she's got no priors, and she's active in the PTA."

"Where's Mr. Bourassa?"

"Dead. County records say he was killed by a truck at an air force base about three years ago."

"What was Mr. Bourassa doing at an air force base?"

I found a small obituary that mentioned Bourassa was a linguist specializing in ancient Indian dialects. Apparently, he was helping translate some Anasazi relics unearthed on air force property near Socorro, New Mexico."

"Huh... Does this Mariah have any family nearby?"

"I don't know yet. No local listing for any other Bourassas, but her maiden name is Aaron, and there are at least a dozen of those. I can't pull her phone records without alerting Darstow, and for similar reasons I can't approach any neighbors."

"Any clue about who was kidnapped?"

"No, and the papers are silent on the matter."

"Okay, cool it for now. Lemme see if I can discover something from my end."

"I'll await your call then?"

"I'll ring tomorrow evening, at five your time."

Thomas sighed. "I wanted to kill him, Dov."

"You've never said why, Thomas."

A long pause followed. And then the line went dead. Dov rubbed his eyes and flicked off the scrambler. He reached for his Manhattan, and began reviewing his notes.

Mariah and Henri Bourassa. He would run routine computer scans on them both first thing in the morning. Neither scan should arouse suspicion.

Dov hoped Darstow hadn't any spies in his Division. But spying was Darstow's business, and Dov had a gnawing suspicion that unless he kept this matter completely to himself, Darstow would discover Dov's involvement.

CHAPTER TEN

Santa Fe, New Mexico

"Director Darstow?"

"What is it?"

"We've picked up a local scrambled transmission."

"Could you identify the source?"

"No, not enough time. All we know is it originated outside New Mexico, was directed somewhere in Santa Fe, and lasted approximately two minutes."

"Does CIA have any operations ongoing here?"

"Not that we're aware of."

"Set up a fast-link array. If there's another transmission, that ought to pinpoint the receiving source."

"Yes sir."

"I want to know about any further transmissions the minute they occur."

"Understood."

* * *

Athens, Greece

Sri Lanka, Cambodia, and Nepal. Andrew ticked them off one by one. In the past three years, an attacking superior force in each of these tiny nations had been rendered impotent by a series of unexpected blinding flashes. The stories of the few surviving attackers had all been remarkably similar to that related by the Chinese helicopter pilot, Gaiyen. A sudden brilliant flash, followed by permanent blindness to the attackers alone.

Neither attackers nor defenders could account for the phenomenon, other than to attribute it to God or the devil. But Gaiyen's instincts were right, thought Andrew. It must be some new technology, like a "Star Wars" system, being used by America. But how could he confirm this? He knew no one in the States, let alone people who might have access to what was undoubtedly a secret weapons program. And then it struck him, like the proverbial light bulb going off in his head. If he couldn't find Americans to confirm his suspicions, he'd set events in motion that might lead their government to unknowingly show its hand.

He picked up the bulky telephone handset near his right elbow and hastily dialed "Senior-Editor" Barton's direct line.

"Barton here."

"Rolly, it's Andy."

"Thought you was on holiday through next week."

"Listen, Rolly, I've got a whoops of a story we could run next week, something bizarre, but real."

"This is the *Tattler*, Andy. You got something real, send it to the *Times*."

"No Rolly – please. We've printed so much unbelievable crap, if we publish something actually true, people will eat it up!"

"You know the rules, Andy. Got to have a Bigfoot or a UFO or one of the Royals."

"We'll dress it up, Rolly. But give this one a chance. I'm coming home early to give you first crack."

"I'll never understand why yer always travelin' about lookin' fer news, Andy. Two fists of Scotch and a sick imagination are all I ever needed to pound out a story."

"I'll be in Friday, Rolly. You run this story on page one, and I'll buy you a case of Glenfiddich."

"Yer a scholar and gen'leman, Sir Andrew."

Andrew hung up, nearly faint from Athens' smoke-choked air. Someday he'd work for a paper whose editorial decisions were based on merit rather than bribes of Scotch. But the bribes were getting him what he wanted, ethics be damned.

CHAPTER ELEVEN

Washington, D.C.

Dov's status as the fourth-ranking agent in the Bureau didn't excuse him from passing through the two security checkpoints guarding the route from the Hoover Building's immense entry to his office. Upon clearing security, he keyed in the electronic entry code allowing him access to his suite, and then quickly made his way to his desk. He was so early that only a skeleton crew of agents and administrative staff was on hand. He figured he would have about forty minutes before he was interrupted with the day's usual business.

He flicked on his PC and typed in the necessary access codes. He then keyed in "Mariah Bourassa, born Mariah Aaron." Three seconds later, the screen flashed:

> "Bourassa, Mariah Aaron. Born December 6, 1964, to Marcus Aaron, Ph.D. [Father history, enter 12648] and Jacqueline Kulick, Ph.D. [Mother history, enter 12640]. A.B., with high distinction, Indiana University, Bloomington, 1985.
>
> "Married Henri Tonty Bourassa, Ph.D., October 10, 1985 [Husband history, enter 12649]. Two children, Brittany, born September 15, 1988 [uninvestigated] and Jacob, born September 19, 1990 [uninvestigated].

"Subject, homemaker until January 4, 1996, when began employment as an alarm monitor with Sonitrol Security, Santa Fe. No known subversive affiliations. Currently resides 1023 E. Paseo Redondo, Santa Fe, New Mexico."

Dov's hair stood on end as he read the last line on the screen:

"Subject interrogated December 17, 1995 [See Father history, enter 12648]."

Dov entered 12648, the key code for Marcus Aaron's history. After nearly fifteen seconds, the screen flashed:

"Access denied. Code 8."

Code 8. That was the highest security rating awarded, reserved for only the most sensitive of material. Despite his high rank in the Bureau, Dov had only seen Code 8 material once, when he was briefly shown the Bureau's closely-guarded file on those who had actually killed President Kennedy.

Under Bureau protocol, only four people were entitled to bestow a Code 8 rating on information: the Director, the Deputy Director, Keenan Darstow, and Dov. However, unlike the Director and his Deputy, who were entitled to access all Code 8 files, Dov and Darstow could only access Code 8 materials that they themselves had classified. Darstow could not access material Dov had classified Code 8, and Dov could not review Code 8 material Darstow had classified, at least not without the consent of the classifying party. Without seeing the file, Dov had no way of knowing who had classified Marcus Aaron's file as Code 8, absent making direct inquiries about the matter to the Director, Deputy Director, or Darstow. And, of course, to do that would have revealed his interest in Darstow's activities in Santa Fe.

Dov typed in the access code for Jacqueline Kulick Aaron. Her history reflected nothing remarkable, other than her impressive credentials as a professor of linguistics, first at the Sorbonne and later at the University of Chicago, where she died from leukemia in 1969. The Aarons had married in 1960.

Dov then typed in "12649," the history code for Henri Tonty Bourassa, Mariah's late husband. The screen flashed:

"Access denied. Code 8."

"Shit!" cursed Dov. He slapped off the PC. It was clear he wasn't going to find what he was looking for through the Bureau's computer systems. He was going to have to hit the street to get some answers.

CHAPTER TWELVE

Taos, New Mexico

The FBI maintains scores of safe houses throughout North America. Most were acquired during the Cold War to secret Soviet bloc defectors for periods sufficient to complete their interrogations. The Bureau had only one safe house in New Mexico, a rambling, territorial-style ranch surrounded by twelve acres of towering cottonwoods just north of Taos. To Thomas's knowledge, it had never been used.

Safe houses were the exclusive domain of the Division of Internal Security, headed by Keenan Darstow, whose presence in Santa Fe might mean there was related activity at the Taos safe house.

Thomas thought it worthwhile to check out the lead.

At any time of the year, the drive from Santa Fe to Taos over the old Taos Highway is breathtaking. The last half of the route follows the turquoise Rio Grande as it winds its way through the fir-packed Sangre de Cristo Mountains. The drive is especially stirring in the fall, and Thomas caught himself smiling as his convertible snaked from one curve to the other, gaining altitude with each passing mile.

It was early evening when he reached the ranch. He parked well down the road, and holstering his SIG P225, crept under the barbwire encircling the perimeter.

Fifty yards from the ranch house, it became clear the safe house was occupied. The west side of the house was lit, although

Thomas couldn't see any moving figures. He crept closer, careful not to trip any alarm wires. As he had been trained, he tried to blend his movements with the natural noises of the night.

Suddenly, the front door shot open, light streamed towards him. Thomas dove into a juniper bush to his left, not five yards from the door. Two men exited, one ran toward the back, the other halted just outside in the center of a circular driveway that separated Thomas from the house. The man reached into his torn pea-coat for a lighter. A cigarette dangled from his lips. Thomas only saw him as a silhouette, for the light coming from the front entrance was too bright to clearly make out his features.

"Hurry up with the friggin' van, Melvin," the smoker shouted.

The voice sounded eerily familiar, thought Thomas. The smoker then turned, re-entered the house, and re-exited leading a blindfolded girl of about eleven. The girl wore a blue jumper, with tattered white leotards and pale blue shoes. The girl tripped over the front step, and the smoker violently yanked her back to her feet as he shut the front door. The girl began to cry. The smoker cuffed her with the back of his hand. "Shut up," he hissed.

Thomas had seen enough. His grip tightened on the butt of his pistol. As he raised his gun for a crippling shot, the smoker's face became recognizable, outlined in the rising moon glow.

Piter Mentol. The IRA assassin. Thomas had once been attached to an SAS team whose mission was to capture or kill him. At the time, they had all remarked how lucky Mentol had been to escape them. With Mentol now using a safe house maintained by Keenan Darstow, it was becoming clear perhaps luck had played no part in the matter.

A white Chrysler van veered from around the back of the house and up the drive toward Mentol. It screeched to a stop. Mentol gathered the girl up like a sack of potatoes, jumped into the front passenger seat, and pressed the girl to his lap. The van raced away. Thomas couldn't make out the driver, but assumed it was the man who had exited the front door with Mentol.

Thomas emerged from his cover and carefully crept along the perimeter of the house, his left side pressed against the exterior wall. It seemed as if the house was empty. Suddenly, a light at the far end of the house came on. Thomas crept towards the area. The room initially lit then darkened and a room next to it brightened. That too went black, and then a third room lit up. It was as if someone was moving from one room to the next, all the while making their way towards Thomas's position. He came upon a French door and attempted to turn the latch. It was locked. A fourth room closer to him lit up, and Thomas decided to stay put to see if the person moving about would come to him.

The room with the French door then brightened, which temporarily blinded him. By the time his sight normalized, he was only able to see the room's inner door slam shut, as if the person inside had seen him.

Thomas retraced his steps. If he'd been seen, he knew he could best escape by hiding himself beside the juniper bush five yards from the front door. He reached the juniper without incident, and gathered its prickly, pungent branches around him. He tried to stifle his rapid breathing. Minutes ticked by.

The front door flew open and a small boy ran out, tears streaming down his cheeks. The boy looked about as if getting his bearings. He started jogging down the drive toward the open highway.

He kept thirty yards behind the boy. It was easy to track him, because the boy was simply heading north on old New Mexico 12, towards Chimayo. Curiously, the boy did not attempt to hitch a ride, but instead, hid in the trees beside the road every time a car approached.

After what seemed like several miles, the boy turned west on an unmarked dirt road. About three hundred yards later, he lay down on a bough of pine needles fallen from a mammoth ponderosa, and cried himself to sleep.

Thomas could smell the boy's despair. He'd stay with him, and guard him from harm. Christ, this was turning into a real Disney movie -- all that was missing was the big, yellow dog.

CHAPTER THIRTEEN

Washington, D.C.

Dov was awed every time he entered the immense circular reading room of the Library of Congress. A soft light filtered through the huge stained-glass dome capping the ceiling eight stories above. Before him lay twenty-four sets of shelves, each exactly six feet high. The first set of shelves was arranged in a circle that spanned 1,500 feet in diameter. Inside the first set lay the remaining sets, each slightly smaller in diameter than its predecessor. They appeared to be spaced about six feet apart, and their radii were uniformly broken to allow for thirteen spoke-like passages leading towards the room's center. There, deep in the recesses of an immense Cray 9000 mainframe, the sum of all published work since recorded history was preserved.

"Good morning sir, may I help you?"

"Yes, thank you. I'm Special Agent Dov Bar-Lev, to see Dr. Pentov."

The young woman glanced down at her computer screen. "Yes, she is waiting for you. Do you know the way?"

"No."

The woman smiled. "Take Spoke 12 to the outer wall, enter the corridor just to the left, and continue until you see a set of elevators. Take the right bank to the 6th Floor, and the guard on station will take you in."

Dov started down Spoke 12 and eventually managed to reach Dr. Beatrice Pentov's office. Seeing his image in the frosted glass door outside her suite, he used his fingers to brush through his dark, thinning hair, which had been mussed by the strong fall winds that had descended upon the Capital.

Man, I need to lose weight, big time.

He knocked. Hearing nothing, he opened the door and peeked in. The decor was surprisingly chic for a government office; black leather furniture trimmed with granite was tastefully arranged around trinkets from Africa and Asia. Packed bookshelves lined the walls.

"Dr. Pentov?" Dov called.

"I'll just be a minute, Agent Bar-Lev." The voice was that of a woman in her early 60s, and appeared to come from a room just outside the reception area.

Dov began pacing the room, looking at the various objects displayed. Many of the books in the shelves were foreign, and nearly all seemed to have been authored by Beatrice Pentov.

He turned just as Dr. Pentov approached him, straightening her colorful, one-piece dress. She was about five feet three inches tall and slightly built, with grey black hair pulled back in a bun. The most stunning turquoise necklace Dov had ever seen encircled her neck.

She clasped his right hand in hers, shook it vigorously, and guided him to an overstuffed leather chair beside a granite coffee table. "I'm so glad you called about Marcus Aaron, Agent Bar-Lev. I miss him terribly, and I hope I can be of help in locating him." She pushed Dov into the chair and then sat opposite him in a black love seat.

"Some tea perhaps, before we begin?"

Dov put up his hand, "No thank you Doctor, my time is short."

"Please, my friends call me Trixie. What would you like to know?"

"On the phone, you told me Dr. Aaron was a renowned linguist, who specialized in ancient tongues."

"Correct. He disappeared three years ago and hasn't been seen since."

"Do you know the circumstances surrounding his disappearance?"

Dr. Pentov rearranged herself, reached across the coffee table, and withdrew a cigarette from an intricately decorated lapis box. "Do you mind if I smoke?" she asked.

Dov shook his head. "Of course not."

"That's what I like, a polite *and* politically incorrect man." She drew on her cigarette, and began. "I first met Marcus in Peru. It was 1958, I think. I was lecturing at a symposium sponsored by the University of Lima. There was a strikingly handsome young man with a shock of jet black hair that attended each of my lectures. He sat in the front row, dead center. I can't deny I wasn't interested in him, and so I was elated when after my closing lecture, he asked to speak with me. Of course, the young man of whom I speak was Dr. Marcus Aaron. Not only was he a wonderful conversationalist, but he could converse in more tongues than I could, and at that time, I believe I spoke nearly seventy languages. What was equally amazing about Marcus was the diversity of his linguistic ability."

"What do you mean -- diversity?"

"Some languages are quite similar to one another, because they have the same roots. For example, French, English, and Spanish are all based upon the Latin alphabet and are closely related in structure and syntax. Consequently, people that can speak one of these languages usually will have little trouble, with some practice, speaking the other two. But to speak all the known languages of the continent, together with many of the African, East Asian, and South Pacific tongues, is really something, especially since most of those are based on radically different alphabets. Marcus could do all that and more -- I was told he even spoke excellent Navajo -- one of the most difficult of all languages to learn. He could even sign, as you would when communicating with the deaf."

"So you would say Dr. Aaron was a genius?"

"He had a gift, there is no doubt. During our first conversation that warm evening in Lima, we amused ourselves by flirting in different languages. I remember feeling totally frustrated that Marcus could easily respond to my inquiries, whether they were in Hindi or Malawi, but that I couldn't respond to some of his, especially those he framed in ancient American Indian dialects."

"Were American Indian languages his specialty?"

"Towards the latter part of his career, yes. After Jacqueline died -- that was his wife -- he tired of traveling abroad, and concentrated his research on compiling a comprehensive dictionary of all Western American Indian languages."

Dov rose and walked to the west window that overlooked the Potomac. "Forgive me doctor, but I must ask this. Were you and Dr. Aaron ever more than just. . . well, professional colleagues?"

Dr. Pentov looked at him pensively. Dov thought she was going to cry, but then she just smiled. "I suppose I have loved Marcus Aaron since the day I met him. I was crushed when he married Jacqueline, and I never understood why after her death, he was unable or unwilling to rekindle the feelings we shared before Jacqueline appeared. Does that answer your question, Agent Bar-Lev?"

Dov felt foolish for having asked. "What do you know of Dr. Aaron's family, particularly his daughter, Mariah, or her late husband, Dr. Henri Bourassa?"

"I've known Mariah since her birth, a lovely, bright girl. Incredibly beautiful, red hair and slim figure. Marcus used to take her with him to conventions and seminars, and we've enjoyed many a dinner together."

"And her husband, Henri Bourassa?"

"Henri was an up-and-coming force in academe, and it wasn't only because of his close association with Marcus Aaron. He was widely-published, known to have significant knowledge of Western American Indian and Far Eastern dialects, which are somewhat related by the way. But like Marcus, he ceased publishing papers in 1996, when Henri and Marcus moved to Socorro, New Mexico, and began working for the air force."

"What do you know of their work?"

"Practically nothing. When Marcus moved to New Mexico, I wrote asking what he was doing there. He responded that his work was secret, and all he had been authorized to say was it involved an effort to translate what they hoped was the Rosetta Stone of the Anasazi."

Dov scratched his head. "What's the Rosetta Stone, and. . . who are the Anasazi?"

"The Rosetta Stone is a piece of carved rock discovered in 1799 by Napoleon's forces as they passed through Egypt. The Stone contained a lengthy account of an ancient king's coronation in three languages -- Latin, Greek and Egyptian Hieroglyphic. Until discovery of the Stone, no definitive translation of Egyptian Hieroglyphic had ever been made because we had no reference point. The accompanying Greek and Latin texts on the Stone helped us to fully understand the

Hieroglyphics of the Pharaohs. It was a phenomenal find at the time."

"What are the Anasazi?"

"I'm a bit weak in that department. From what I gathered from Marcus, the Anasazi were a large American Indian tribe that inhabited parts of what are now Arizona, New Mexico, Colorado, and Utah about 2,000 years ago. Apparently, their civilization was quite advanced, similar to that of the Aztecs. Remarkably, all traces of the Anasazi abruptly end about 20 A.D. -- Marcus told me that anthropologists haven't a clue as to what happened to the entire lot. In fact, the name Anasazi was bestowed by later Indian peoples. It means, "The Ones Who Disappeared.""

Dov's eye once again fell on Dr. Pentov's turquoise necklace. She recognized his glance and said, "It's beautiful, isn't it?"

"I've never seen anything like it."

"I put this on because you were coming to talk about Marcus. He sent this to me by parcel post just before he disappeared. A friend of mine at the Smithsonian Metallurgical Department inspected it and claims it's not only ancient, but that the metal enclosing the stones is of unknown makeup and origin."

"Remarkable. When Dr. Aaron sent you the necklace, did he include a note?"

"Yes, I still have it. Wait a second." Dr. Pentov rose and hurried into a room adjoining the reception area. She returned with a well-worn piece of light blue note paper. She fumbled for her reading glasses, which were hanging from a beaded chain around her thin neck. She perched the bifocals at the tip of her nose and read:

"Dearest Trixie:

"Only you could appreciate this. Treasure it, and perhaps it will someday bring us together.

"Marcus"

"What does it mean?"

"I've spent countless sleepless nights asking myself the same question. At first I thought it was a love note, but now, well. . . I'm not sure. It's been over three years, and he still hasn't come through that door." Pentov handed the note to Dov.

"May I keep this note for a couple of days?"

"Of course."

"Do you know anything of Henri Bourassa's death?"

Dov walked to the window, admiring the view.

"Just what was in the papers, and what I learned from Mariah at Henri's funeral. I guess he was killed by a runaway fuel truck at an air force base, about the same time Marcus disappeared. I wasn't very close to Henri, because I suspected Mariah resented my presence. It was no secret I sought her father's attention."

Dov had learned all he could. "Thank you Doctor, I truly appreciate your time."

"I'm going to bend you over my knee and give you a good spanking if you don't start calling me Trixie."

Dov laughed, and put up his hands, as if surrendering.

"Okay Trixie. Thanks again."

As Dov turned for the door, Trixie asked, "Why are you interested in Marcus, Agent Bar-Lev?"

Dov chuckled. "You know, I'm not sure. Good day."

CHAPTER FOURTEEN

Taos, New Mexico

Thomas awoke with a start, as a large black beetle crawled up his leg. He shook the beetle away and stood to see if the boy was still under the tree thirty feet to his right.

Thank heavens the boy's still there.

He slowly maneuvered within three feet of the boy and sat down opposite him. "Good morning," he said in the most cheerful tone he could muster. The boy shot up like a Roman candle, his eyes wider than saucers. He was about to bolt, but Thomas didn't rise. Instead, Thomas just raised his arms, palms outward, as if he was a criminal giving up to the authorities.

"Please son, don't run away. I'm not one of the bad guys."

The boy backpedaled. "How...how do I know?" The boy's eyes were fixed on Thomas's holstered gun.

In one fluid motion, Thomas drew the gun, removed its magazine, and tossed the gun to the ground at the boy's feet. "Take it -- but, by God, be careful, it still has one bullet in the chamber, so don't squeeze the trigger."

The boy eyed the gun suspiciously. He lunged down, grabbed the gun, and pointed it at Thomas.

"The first thing you have to learn when holding a gun is *never* rest your finger on the trigger," Thomas lectured. "Straighten your finger along the side of the gun adjacent to the trigger but not resting on it. That will prevent an accidental discharge."

To Thomas's surprise, the boy complied.

"Who are you?" the boy asked.

"My name is Thomas Kuzmic – I'm a private investigator."

"Like on TV?"

"Just like on TV, except not so handsome."

"How did you find me?" The boy kept the barrel of the gun pointed directly at Thomas's chest.

I was hiding in some bushes just outside the house. I saw Piter Mentol exit the house with a young girl. He then drove away with her in a white van driven by another man I couldn't identify."

"Melvin," offered the boy.

"And then I saw you leave, and I followed you here."

"Why were you at the house?" The boy's breath was clearly visible in the morning chill.

Thomas paused. "My best friend in the world is a man named Dov – he's a special kind of policeman in Washington D.C. He heard there was someone kidnapped in Santa Fe, and he asked me to find out who was taken, and why." Thomas's voice softened. "I think you were taken son, and the girl. Perhaps you can tell me why?"

The boy smiled. "They took Brittany and me when we were sleeping. They drove us out to the house, and kept us in separate rooms."

"What's your name?"

"Jacob."

"Jacob who?"

"Jacob Bourassa."

"How old are you?"

Jacob lowered the gun. "Nine, ten, almost."

"And Brittany is your sister?"

"Yeah. She's eleven."

"Do you know why you and Brittany were kidnapped?"

"No. Piter didn't talk much, and Melvin just yelled a lot."

"What would Melvin yell about?"

Jacob's eyes flashed with pride. "Mostly, at me, 'cause I would use Ninja on him whenever he came into my room."

"How come Piter and Melvin left you in the house when they drove away with Brittany?"

Jacob related how he had hidden in the lodge-pole ceiling, and then searched the house for Brittany after his captors left.

"That was smart," Thomas said. "Want some breakfast?"

"I want to go home." Jacob again pointed the gun at Thomas's chest.

"If you return home, you'll be taken again, or worse. Although I don't have proof of this yet, I believe that Piter and Melvin work for one of the most powerful policemen in the world, a man named Darstow. At this very minute, he's with your mom *pretending* to investigate your kidnapping."

"If he's a policeman, why did he take us?" Jacob sat, perplexed.

"He's the worst kind of policeman, Jacob. A corrupt one. And as for why he took you, I honestly don't know. Let's hike back to my car and get some breakfast in Chimayo. Then we'll figure out our next move." Thomas extended his hand for the gun. Jacob didn't move.

"If I wanted to harm you, I could have done so while you were sleeping; and I certainly wouldn't have given you my gun."

After a few moments, Jacob put the gun down on a stump to his right. "Okay, you can have your gun back, but remember I have special Ninja powers."

Thomas laughed as he reinserted the magazine and then holstered the SIG.

"Son, what you got is what my friend Dov would call Chutzpah."

CHAPTER FIFTEEN

Santa Fe, New Mexico

The headline in the *Tattler* screamed: U.S. USES STAR WARS! Darstow pulled the tabloid closer to better read the text:

"By Andrew Sawyer, special correspondent.

"Dateline, Nepal: Highly placed sources in the U.S. defense establishment have confirmed reports that the U.S. Air Force has used space-based laser beams to disrupt attacks from anti-democratic forces in Sri Lanka, Cambodia, and Nepal.

"Suspicions that the Americans were actually using so called "Star Wars" technology first arose in August, when witnesses reported that a Tamil rebel attack was foiled by a blinding flash of light originating from the sky. According to investigators at the scene, only the rebels were affected by the light beam, which lasted less than a second and permanently blinded the entire rebel force. A similar incident was reported in Cambodia three months ago, where remnants of Khmer Rouge forces were routed by several bursts of bright light emanating from the clouds. And as recently as last month, an entire brigade of China's elite 8th Airwing was destroyed by a white hot beam just as the Chinese forces were about to storm a Tibetan rebel stronghold near the village of Pratmankun on the Nepal border.

"The sole surviving Chinese attacker, a Captain Gaiyen, told investigators that he watched in horror as two of his sister attack helicopters crashed after being hit by bursts of incredibly bright light from an unknown source. Gaiyen's gunship then crashed after Gaiyen himself became blinded by a white flash. The Captain remains totally blind, and is being held for ransom by rebel forces.

"The Chinese government has lodged a strident protest with the American embassy, demanding an explanation for the attack on its gunships, which it maintains were on a humanitarian mission. Both the White House and the State Department deny any American involvement. However, high level sources in the U.S. Air Force have confirmed that the white flashes are laser beams generated by scores of American nuclear powered satellites that now span the globe.

"While the satellites have pinpoint accuracy, they are incapable of destroying anything. Instead, they are designed to blind the pilots of slow flying aircraft such as helicopters and subsonic fighters. The lasers are also capable of blinding large groups of ground forces, as occurred in Cambodia and Sri Lanka. The implications of this new weapon are far reaching. Troops and pilots alike will now have to be equipped with special eye protection to prevent becoming permanently blinded by the new space-based lasers."

Darstow threw the paper to the table. "This garbage may serve our purposes well by diverting attention away from our operation." He turned toward Mentol, a glint in his eye. "Let's give the *Tattler* some well-deserved credibility, Mr. Mentol. Pay a friendly visit to the idiot who wrote this piece, and lead him to believe he's on to something."

Mentol nodded, and turned to leave.

"And, Mr. Mentol."

Mentol turned back.

"Your visit should be no secret."

CHAPTER SIXTEEN

Santa Fe, New Mexico

Thomas heard the familiar hiss, as Dov's scrambler kicked in. "Good evening, goyim." Dov greeted him.
"Don't be a schmuck. I've got a hell of a lot to tell you."
"Ditto. You first."
Thomas related his encounters with Mentol and Jacob.
"So Mentol and an associate have kidnapped Mariah Bourassa's children, very likely on Keenan Darstow's orders. Does anyone know you have Jacob?"
"Only you. Got any ideas?"
"It would be crazy to return Jacob. Darstow would simply have him taken again, and he'd probably have you fingered as one of the kidnappers. Is there any way you can connect up with Mariah, let her know what's going on, without alerting Darstow?"
"I'll give it some thought. What did you find out?"
"It turns out Mariah's father, Dr. Marcus Aaron, was a language expert, specializing in ancient American Indian languages. He and his son-in-law and colleague, Professor Henri Bourassa, were attempting to decipher some Anasazi writings at a New Mexico air base when Bourassa was killed and Aaron disappeared. An old flame, a Dr. Beatrice Pentov, said Aaron believed he was on the verge of a major breakthrough of some kind at the time he began working out of the small air force base near Socorro, New Mexico."

"Did this Dr. Pentov know why Aaron and Bourassa were working for the air force, or why they were stationed in Socorro?"

"She tried to find out, but Aaron said his work was secret. That was no joke. Aaron and Bourassa's Bureau files are rated Code 8."

Thomas gasped, as Dov continued. "All Aaron would tell Pentov was that he was on the verge of finding a new 'Rosetta Stone.'"

"That's interesting. Did Pentov tell you how she found out Aaron had disappeared?"

"She was in semi-regular contact with the family, and attended Bourassa's funeral. Wait a minute.... About a week before Bourassa died and Aaron vanished, Pentov received a very unusual turquoise necklace in the mail, from Aaron. Pentov said the Smithsonian has tested the metal holding the turquoise stones and get this-- it is of unknown makeup and origin."

"No kidding? What the heck does that mean?"

"Beats me. But it gets even more interesting. Listen to the note accompanying the necklace:

> "Dearest Trixie:
>
> Only you could appreciate this. Treasure it, and perhaps it will someday bring us together.
> Marcus"

"The note must be linked to Aaron's disappearance."

"Agreed. It sounds to me that Aaron planned to vanish, and that the necklace provides some guide to finding him."

"Does Pentov come to the same conclusion?"

"Yes, although she can't unravel its hidden message."

"Sounds to me like you ought to have the lab and cryptology boys do a number on that note and necklace."

"Can't do that yet. Pentov never showed the note to anyone but the Smithsonian and me, and if I ask the Bureau to do a work up on them, Darstow will hear about it."

"Do you have the note or the jewelry?"

"She lent me the note, but I was hesitant to ask for the necklace. It seemed to have great sentimental value to her."

"Just the same, maybe we could decipher something from the necklace -- why don't you see if you can borrow it too?"

"It's worth a shot. I'll visit her again tomorrow. In the meantime, keep the boy safe. You got a backup station?"

"If things get sticky, look for us at Old Vic's."

"What's the name of that lake it's on?"

"Medicine Stone."

"Same time tomorrow, Tonto."

"Okay, Kimosabe."

Thomas glanced across his study at Jacob, who was fast asleep on the torn leather couch crowding the opposite wall. *Probably the first good sleep the little bugger has enjoyed since being nabbed.* Thomas tripped the light and headed upstairs to bed, oblivious that death was only sixteen minutes away.

CHAPTER SEVENTEEN

Santa Fe, New Mexico

They'd run the routine scores of times. AD Darstow had assured them that the target was a known terrorist, implicated in the TWA 800 downing just a few years earlier. The AD made it clear -- take the perp down, alive, if possible. When push came to shove, that "if" was likely to get lost in the shuffle.

They fanned out around the house: two to each window, with three-man squads at the front and rear doors. Every agent dressed in SWAT black, wearing full vesting and silent communications links.

They were to perform a standard "Blow In" when they heard the third tone over their earpieces. Everyone was nearly in place.

* * *

Thomas was too tired to undress. Instead, he crashed onto the bed, not even bothering to pull down the covers. The evening was especially quiet. Though dead tired, he couldn't stop thinking about Marcus Aaron, the mysterious note, and unique necklace. What did it all mean?

Omar cackled.

Thomas shot up. Omar was furiously pacing back and forth in his cage, cackling and pecking as never before.

The Arabian pigeon is as unremarkable as other varieties of its species, with one notable exception -- in the range of 300 to 460 decibels, the bird's hearing is far more sensitive than any dog. Human breathing lies almost exclusively within that range; and for centuries, Arabian pigeons had acted as a sort of early warning radar to the Bedouin, who often fell prey to thieves of the night.

Thomas grabbed his keys and reached under the dresser for his backup gun. Not bothering to hunt for his coat, he hurled himself down the stairs and into the study, where Jacob still lay curled on the couch. Thomas scooped the boy into his arms, hoisted him onto his shoulder, and pulled open the door to the cellar. And then the front door blew off.

CHAPTER EIGHTEEN

Santa Fe, New Mexico

"Dear Mariah," it began.

"I so enjoyed our visit together last fall. I especially remember that lovely lunch we had at La Tortulia and our obscene shopping spree at the Nambe outlet store. With the economy as it is, I imagine you can get even better bargains there this year. I still wish I had bought that large, irregularly shaped serving bowl, the one that looked sort of like an inverted, three-cornered hat. Oh well, perhaps I'll get it next time I drop in.

"Your Uncle Richard is doing fine. I visit him twice a week at the home, where they do the best they can with him. I busy myself with my cooking and needlework, and it would be wonderful if you and the children could visit me. It would give me a chance to see if I'm still the best cook in the family. All my love, dear.

"Elsa"

Mariah let the note fall to her lap. She smiled, thinking of her Aunt Elsa. The dear old woman was a favorite, not only for her considerable talents in the kitchen, but for her kind heart and gentle manner. It was Elsa who acted as her surrogate mother after Jacqueline died, and she missed her terribly. But, of course, she could never see Elsa again, for the frail, gentle lady died many years ago.

Mariah felt her blood pressure rise. Who could have sent the note? Could this be someone's bizarre idea of a joke? She didn't recognize the handwriting, although it appeared feminine. The postmark was from Chicago, where Elsa lived during her last years. The note was dated four days ago. She flushed with anger.

What a sick prank.

Disgusted, she threw the note in the trash bin and fell into bed.

How much more torment can I bear?

As she had done so many nights before, she swallowed two sleeping pills and hoped sleep would soon overcome her.

* * *

She awoke with a start. The clock by the bed stand read 9:40 a.m., nearly two hours later than the time she usually awoke. She pushed away the sheets and spun out of bed, nearly stepping on Muffin, Brittany's brown Lhasa Apso.

God, what a headache.

She stumbled toward the bathroom, thinking again about the note.

Elsa never visited the Nambe store, much less lunched with me at La Tortulia. Now, Dad and I ate there...*oh my God.*

She rushed to the trash can where she had tossed the note, and read it again. Nambe. La Tortulia.

Both were Dad's favorites. *Is this some sort of code? Am I supposed to visit the restaurant or store for further instructions?*

For the first time since the children had been taken weeks earlier, she felt she was doing something to achieve their rescue. She dressed quickly, in jeans and an over-large white T-shirt tucked in at her slim waist. She grabbed her bag and opened her bedroom door, only to be greeted by this day's minders, agents Russo and Leland.

"Going out?" Russo raised his bushy eyebrows.

"Just sick and tired of waiting for the phone to ring," Mariah answered, with a thin smile. "Thought I'd do some shopping, get some air."

Russo nodded and motioned for Leland to get his car, a late model white Ford Taurus. Mariah had learned it was no use attempting to go alone. The agents insisted on escorting her everywhere.

Leland pulled the car up to the curb. Russo opened the rear left passenger door for Mariah, and then crowded his massive frame into the compact's front passenger seat, and they drove off for the square.

* * *

Santa Fe is one of the oldest cities in the United States. At various times over the centuries, the Spanish, Mexican, Confederate, and Union flags had flown over the city's central square, which that afternoon was littered with thousands of amber, gold, red, and brown leaves from the massive oak trees surrounding it. To the immediate north, running the entire length of the square, was the Palace of Governors, itself this nation's oldest government building. Under the eaves of the Palace, seated shoulder-to-shoulder, were scores of local Indians selling handmade jewelry and crafts.

La Tortulia was not open until eleven-thirty, so Mariah directed Russo to the Nambe outlet store, which was a half mile further south. "No need to come in," Mariah pleaded. "I'm just going to look for some replacement pieces."

"Sorry," said Leland. "You know our orders. One of us has to stay with you at all times." They pulled into the Nambe lot, and Leland leapt from the car to open Mariah's door.

Realizing Mariah's discomfort with being shadowed, Leland kept his distance in the shop. Now that she was here, however, she didn't know what to do. Bewildered, she walked through the rows of gleaming steel bowls, candlesticks and platters, pretending to shop.

"May I help you, miss?" The inquiry came from a primly dressed, tall woman to her immediate right.

"Uh, I'm looking for an unusual bowl I saw in here last year. It sort of looks like a three-cornered hat."

The saleswoman looked momentarily startled. "Oh, I think I have the piece you're interested in. Could you wait a minute? I think it's in the stockroom."

"Of course."

As the saleswoman walked to the stockroom at the rear of the store, Mariah tried her best to look composed, as if this really was just a normal outing. To her relief, Agent Leland appeared to be ignoring her.

Suddenly, she felt a hand on her left forearm. Momentarily startled, she recoiled backward, almost knocking over a tower of glass display shelves.

"I'm so sorry," the saleswoman exclaimed, who had returned with a brown cardboard box under her left arm. "I have a bad habit of sneaking up on people." She looked at Mariah, her eyes searching for forgiveness.

"Think nothing of it. I have a bad habit of letting people sneak up on me." Mariah didn't recognize the irony of her statement until she had uttered it.

"Well, I'm sure this is the bowl you are looking for," said the saleswoman, directing her glance to the box under her arm. "Three-cornered, just as you said."

"Could I see it?" Mariah asked, gesturing for the bowl to be removed from the box.

"Of course." The saleswoman set the box on the floor between them and pulled out the bowl, which truly did look like an inverted tri-cornered hat. Like all Nambe goods, it was polished steel with rounded edges.

The saleswoman grasped Mariah by the forearm, and wrenched her nearer, whispering, "This piece will look especially well at your bedside, my dear." She emphasized the word "bedside" as she dropped the bowl into the box and brought it to the cash register, where she taped up the box.

Agent Leland joined Mariah at the sales counter. Mariah reached for her wallet. The saleswoman laughed and patted her hand. "This had already been paid for."

Mariah stared back blankly.

"Oh yes, here it is." The saleswoman reached for a yellow invoice, taped to the box. "Paid for by your Aunt Elsa."

Mariah smiled, trying not to look surprised, although she could feel her pulse racing. "That trickster. Always surprising the family with gifts. Well, thank you for being so helpful." As she turned, Leland looked at her quizzically.

"Who is Aunt Elsa?"

"A dear old woman who always thinks more of others than herself," she replied. "Take me home, will you? I don't feel up to lunch."

CHAPTER NINETEEN

Santa Fe, New Mexico

The concussion tossed them down half the flight of stairs. Luckily, Thomas landed on his side, with the boy trapped between Thomas's back and the right handrail. Plaster dust rolled down the stairwell.

We only have a few moments before being caught by...well, whoever.

He tried to ignore the sharp pain in his left side and head, wrenched Jacob loose, grabbed him by his back belt-loop, and stumbled down the landing towards his fort.

Ever since his days as a counterintelligence agent, Thomas had made sure that each of his dwellings had a "fort," an impenetrable room with arms, food, communications equipment, and most importantly, an escape route accessible only from the room's interior. If he could reach his fort, perhaps his significant life-saving investment would prove worthwhile.

The fort was essentially a six-by-eight foot ventilated safe, built by the Wolf Schmidt Company of Switzerland. Its tempered steel walls were half a foot thick. The fort abutted the east wall of the basement, and was accessed by a huge door with a small electronic keypad at its center. Once locked from the inside, the outside keypad became disabled. Choking on the clouds of thick plaster-dust that poured into the basement, Thomas frantically punched in the access code. Above his head, sounds of men stepping purposefully through the house increased his sense of urgency.

A concussion grenade bounced down the stairwell as Thomas heard the bolts to the fort's door slide open. With all his remaining strength, Thomas yanked the massive door open, dragged the boy inside, and pulled the door shut behind him. Milliseconds later, as Thomas engaged the door's locking mechanism, the concussion grenade exploded, having little effect other than startling them.

The fort's interior lit up as they entered. Ignoring Jacob's persistent crying, Thomas switched on the closed-circuit video camera perched above the fort. At first, he saw nothing but plaster dust. Out of the cloud, two figures, each dressed in SWAT battle-dress, appeared through the haze. Thomas instantly recognized the men as FBI "HRT," an acronym for Hostage Rescue Team, the Bureau's elite special weapons and tactics outfit.

Dov's suspicions were now confirmed; these men were undoubtedly operating under Keenan Darstow's command.

Thomas figured he had no more than twenty minutes before his pursuers amassed sufficient plastique to blow the fort's door. He turned to his right and punched the digits on another electronic keypad adjacent to a metal cabinet welded to the wall. A small lock at the base of the cabinet gave way revealing several scoped rifles, an Uzi submachine gun, an HK SP-89 automatic rifle, and numerous semi-automatic handguns. Thomas chose the Uzi, the HK, and a SIG-Sauer P226, a nine-millimeter semi-automatic handgun with a fifteen-round magazine. He opened an ammo box situated immediately below the gun cabinet, and scooped up four loaded magazines for each weapon. A nearby box contained three bundles of $50 bills, each with a $1000 wrapper. Thomas stuffed the money into a rucksack, along with the SIG P226, the ammo clips, a halogen flashlight, four bricks of C-4 plastic explosive, their accompanying detonators, and a large multi-purpose knife that had been hanging on the opposite wall.

Jacob stopped crying. "Can I have a gun?"

"Not until you learn how to use one. But I do need your help. Can I count on you?"

The boy's face hardened. "Just tell me what you want me to do."

"Open that cabinet to your left, the one with the metal handle."

Jacob complied, revealing a small cache of freeze dried meats, granola bars, vitamin packets, and medicines. Thomas threw the boy a camouflage-patterned rucksack. "Stuff this with as many things as you can." Thomas didn't wait for a response. He punched in several numbers on a nearby keypad, and then turned his attention to the far end of the fort, which appeared to be nothing but a bare steel wall. Slowly, the lower third of the wall rose, revealing a dark passage broken only by a wooden ladder leading down a vertical shaft.

Thomas punched another set of codes into the keypad, and said, "We're out of here, kid. Let's go." Jacob hadn't finished stuffing the rucksack when Thomas grabbed him by the arm and nearly threw him toward the dark opening.

"I'm not done yet," he protested.

Thomas glared at him. "We have thirty seconds to get through that escape hatch before it closes. And when it closes, nothing short of thirty sticks of dynamite is going to open it again. So get off your butt and get down that shaft!" Thomas screamed.

It was difficult climbing down the wooden ladder carrying the guns and supplies, and Thomas nearly slipped a couple of times on the dirty rungs. He had never taken the time to run lights through the interior of the shaft, and he was now sorry he hadn't. Jacob scrambled down the ladder without incident, his rucksack thrown casually over his right shoulder.

As Thomas reached the base of the ladder, the fort's escape hatch slammed behind them. He hoped it was as impregnable as the manufacturer had represented.

"Where are we?" the boy asked. His mouth was open, and his eyes wide in amazement.

"This is an unmapped shaft of an old turquoise mine. I first found the shaft, and when I learned it lead directly under this house, I purchased the home and built the access shaft we just climbed down."

"This is really cool," Jacob sputtered. "I can't wait to tell the guys about this."

"Well, if we can get out of here alive, I imagine you'll have a lot of good yarns to tell. Now come on." With that, Thomas flicked on his powerful flashlight, and together, they jogged down the dark passageway, dodging the many large rocks that littered the mine's floor.

After about a quarter of a mile, they came to what appeared to be a dead end. Jacob started back the way they came, but Thomas called him back. "Help me move these rocks. I put them here on purpose to block the exit."

They managed to clear a hole through the wall in less than fifteen minutes. With bleeding hands, Jacob climbed through first and Thomas followed. "Should we put the rocks back?"

"No need. We can never go back to the house, and no one will be able to access the fort from this end."

Thomas walked over to a pile of large boulders to his right. Jacob watched in amazement as Thomas seized several huge boulders and threw them aside to reveal a large black motorcycle covered with a brown sheet that matched the color of the boulders. Thomas winked at Jacob. "I wish I was that strong kid. They're plastic rocks."

The motorcycle was a Yamaha V-Max, outfitted with a black custom faring and black leather saddlebags. Thomas stuffed the rucksacks into the saddlebags and slipped the automatic rifles into sheaths attached to the cycle's sides. He then straddled the bike, ordering Jacob to sit behind him.

"Ever ride a bike before, kid?"

"Uh, sure, all the time." From his tone, Thomas knew this was going to be Jacob's first ride.

"This is the most powerful production motorcycle in the world. So, you have to follow a few new rules, okay?"

The boy squeaked his assent.

"First, always hold me tight, around the waist." Jacob complied.

"And never put your feet down from the pegs they're resting on until I give you the go ahead. Got that?"

"Yep."

Thomas set the ignition key to 'Run.'

"God I hope this baby starts." With that, he depressed the electronic ignition. To his relief, the engine caught. He let it run for thirty seconds.

"Ready for the ride of your life?" Thomas yelled over the roar of the four-stroke engine. He felt the boy squeeze his waist. Thomas eased off the clutch, and together they roared out of the passage into the night.

CHAPTER TWENTY

Santa Fe, New Mexico

She had been so excited, at first. As soon as she returned home, she bid her leave of Russo and Leland and ensconced herself in her bedroom. There, as quietly as she could, she removed the bowl from the box, searching its surface for some clue, some message from her father.

At first, she saw nothing. She pressed her fingers against the bowl's surface, hoping to feel something her eyes had failed to identify. And, almost as if by magic, it appeared at the very bottom of the bowl. The Sign.

It appeared so quickly, Mariah dropped the bowl to the carpet, where it landed with a dull thud. She quickly retrieved it, but just as she again caught sight of the Sign, it began to fade. In a matter of seconds, it completely disappeared.

She rubbed the bowl's underside for hours, hoping to make the Sign reappear. She then tried to heat the bowl in the oven, and when that didn't produce any results, she iced it. Nothing seemed to coax the Sign back, however, and she eventually gave up.

She set the bowl on the nightstand beside her bed. Drained from the morning's venture, she decided to take a nap. Perhaps the key to coaxing the Sign back would become clear after she rested.

"You must call Trixie."

Mariah smiled. This was such a strange dream. In it, her father's head was poised several inches above the tri-cornered bowl, slowly revolving counterclockwise and whispering instructions.

"Trixie has the gift."

What gift? She wondered.

"The gift will find me."

This was so real – so clear. Like no other dream she ever had.

"Where are you Dad?"

"Trust no one."

"Dad, where are you?"

"Especially Darstow."

Her father's head repeated its message, over and over, never directly responding to her inquiries. The head grew silent. She turned toward the bowl, knowing, before she opened her eyes, that she would see nothing.

She was wrong.

CHAPTER TWENTY-ONE

Washington, D.C.

Dov tried to reach Thomas four times. The first three calls had gone unanswered. On the fourth call, however, someone had lifted the receiver, but said nothing. Dov immediately hung up, knowing Thomas would have uttered a greeting.

He felt the adrenaline rush he used to get when on assignment. Thomas was blown.

He dialed Dr. Pentov's private line.

"Hello."

"Dr. Pentov?"

"Agent Bar-Lev. How nice to speak with you so soon."

"I can't believe you recognized my voice."

She laughed. "Just a trick of the trade, I guess."

Knowing time was his enemy, Dov got right to the point. "Doctor, if you wouldn't mind, I would like to borrow the necklace Dr. Aaron sent you. We've got a laboratory in Santa Fe that would like a look at it," he lied.

"How remarkable. Mariah Bourassa just called and invited me to visit her in Santa Fe. And she specifically asked me to bring Marcus's gift."

"Did she say 'gift,' or did she ask for the necklace, specifically by name?"

"She said she was incredibly lonely. That with Henri dead and Marcus missing, I was the closest thing to family she had and, despite our past differences, would I consider visiting for a few days. And then, as if it was an afterthought, she asked if I would bring Marcus's gift."

"Did you question her what that gift might be?"

"No. I just assumed it was the necklace."

"Did you ever tell Mariah about the necklace, Doctor?"

There was a pause. "Come to think of it, I don't think I ever mentioned it. In fact, I'm sure I didn't, because I thought Mariah might resent the fact Marcus was sending me presents."

"Doctor, how long has it been since you spoke with Mariah?"

"Not since Henri's funeral, three years ago."

Dov's mind raced. "Doctor, could I accompany you to Santa Fe?"

"How nice. When shall we leave?"

There was a short pause. "Tonight."

CHAPTER TWENTY-TWO

London, England

Andrew sensed danger the instant he turned on the light. The flat was a wreck, clothes and knickknacks strewn everywhere. All of his pictures had been ripped off the wall and tossed to the floor like so much rubbish.

"Don't move." Andrew nearly jumped through the ceiling in fright. The voice was northern Irish, and menacing.

A gun barrel was positioned against his right ear. "Hands up, fren," the Irishman said.

Andrew raised his shaky arms and starred at the opposite wall. A pair of large hands patted him down.

"Clen," said another voice, this one east-end.

"Turn slowly to yer right, fren," the Irishman said.

Andrew complied, becoming more frightened with each passing moment. Two very stocky men of average height stood before him. They wore pea-coats like those fancied by the merchant marine. Except both carried guns with long silencers.

"Sit," the Irishman said.

There was no place to sit. Sensing his dilemma, the Irishman stepped forward and pushed Andrew into the pile of debris that littered the center of the flat.

Nearly scared out of his wits, Andrew pleaded, "Please, I've got a little money. You can have it all."

The men laughed and grinned at each other.

"It's not yer money we're after," the Irishman said. He took a step closer. "No, it's yer mouth that's a problem." He looked at Andrew with piercing green eyes, searching for some clue that Andrew understood his meaning.

"I don't know what you mean," Andrew bleated.

The Irishman looked at his companion, who was furiously drawing on a bent Marlboro. "Hear that, Melvin?" the Irishman said. "Doesn't know what we mean?"

Melvin grunted, stubbed his cigarette out on a wall and fumbled through his pockets for another.

Before he had time to react, the Irishman seized Andrew by the lapels of his sweat-soaked jacket and slapped him twice in the face. He then threw Andrew to the east wall of the flat, where the portly journalist crashed into an old desk. As Andrew attempted to stand, Melvin stepped forward and kicked him in the stomach, nearly causing him to pass out. Melvin then grabbed Andrew by his thinning red hair, and yanked him to a standing position before the Irishman.

The Irishman leaned toward Andrew's left ear, whispering, "Yer writing things better left unsaid." He raised his black revolver, cocked the hammer and placed the barrel within five centimeters of Andrew's right eye.

"No more stories of lasers and such," the Irishman whispered.

Andrew clamped his eyes shut. He shook uncontrollably.

"No more stories, right?"

Andrew nodded his head.

"Good," the Irishman shouted, almost cheerfully. "Otherwise, we'd be visitin' ya agin." Andrew opened his eyes as both men exited the flat.

He didn't move for several minutes after they had gone. As confirmation he was on the right track, he had hoped for some reaction from the American defense or state departments, possibly some discrete diplomatic effort to derail his investigation, or a news release deriding the irresponsibility of the British tabloids. Instead, he had been beaten and threatened by an east-end thug and his Irish master.

Maybe the Americans know I couldn't be bought off. Maybe political pressure will only encourage me. Do they think I fear for my life? *Maybe they're right.*

Andrew felt dejected. He had absolutely no proof the Americans had hired these men. But if not the Americans, who had the technology to deploy such weapons systems?

The flat was beginning to look better. Andrew got a broom and began to sweep up the glass shards and shredded upholstery. Then he spotted it, a small white and brown matchbook cover. He flipped it over with his foot. The cover read, *The Little Green Men*, below which was pictured what seemed to be three green aliens. Below the aliens was written in large black type, "Roswell, N.M."

Andrew smiled as he snatched up the matchbook. The smoking thug named Melvin must have tossed it.

He hurried over to his library, hoping his atlas had not been one of the casualties of his visitors' rampage. Happily, it was still in the shelves, and he quickly paged to the map of New Mexico, United States. Roswell…Roswell. There it was.

CHAPTER TWENTY-THREE

Santa Fe, New Mexico

The phone rang just as Agent Darstow was leaving. He waited at the door as Mariah ran to pick up the receiver.

"Hello."

"It's me."

She immediately recognized the voice as that of the man who had taken Brittany and Jacob.

"Are they all right?" she pleaded.

"Would you like to speak with the girl?"

"Yes, oh yes." Mariah was thrilled to speak with her daughter.

"Mommy?"

"Yes, darling. Are you okay?"

"Yea. They won't let me go outside."

"You'll soon be home, with me. Is your brother okay?"

"I haven't seen him since we were taken."

A wave of anxiety washed over her. "Brittany, where are you?"

"A house."

"No, honey, where is the house?"

"I don't know. They...."

"It is useless to inquire further about our location," the kidnapper broke in. "Suffice it to say, we'll be gone from this place within a matter of minutes. The boy is safe and well, and both children will be returned after you introduce us to the Professor." The line died.

Mariah was filled with a sense of dread. Brittany had not seen Jacob since the kidnapping. She sensed that the kidnapper's assurances about Jacob's health were not genuine. What if they had hurt her son! She cried, tears streaming from her eyes.

She felt a comforting hand on her shoulder.

"We were unable to fix their position," Darstow murmured. He gently lifted the receiver from Mariah's hand and replaced it on the phone base. For the first time, he looked tired and forlorn.

"I think Jacob might be hurt," Mariah sobbed, and dabbed her eyes.

"Why do you think that?" Darstow replied, a slight hint of surprise in his voice.

"The man seemed evasive when I asked about Jacob."

"I overheard most of the conversation," Darstow countered, and I didn't get that impression at all."

"I hope you're right." Mariah glared at Darstow. "What have you done to get my children back?"

The FBI man walked over to the French doors overlooking the inner courtyard. He paused quite a while before he spoke.

"You know full well we're doing everything we can to get them back." Then suddenly, he turned toward her, fixing her with a cold, blunt stare. "The Professor will contact you before he arrives. You must let me know his intentions. If you don't, your children will surely die."

Mariah was completely taken aback. She flushed, as if he had caught her in a lie.

She felt so confused. Perhaps, if she didn't tell the FBI about her father's holographic message, Brittany and Jacob might be hurt. But her father had specifically told her not to trust anyone, especially Darstow.

"I will do everything you ask to get the children back." She glared at Darstow, in defiance of his icy stare.

The FBI man's face softened. "I know you will, my dear." He tried to place his large arms about her shoulders, but Mariah shrank away, seeking refuge in her bedroom.

"She's up to something. Don't let your guard down for a moment."

Russo nodded.

"And find that boy."

CHAPTER TWENTY-FOUR

Washington, D.C.

It had been a long while since Dov had flown coach on a commercial airline. While he had a Lear at his beck-and-call, he could not use it for fear of tipping off Darstow. As a result, he was crowded into the middle seat, sandwiched between Trixie Pentov, who had the window, and a huge bearded man who, Dov estimated, hadn't bathed in at least a week.

Trixie fell asleep immediately after the meal. As usual, he had forgotten to buy a book to read for the flight. The material in the in-flight magazine held no fascination for him. So he found himself day dreaming, trying to make some sense of what he knew.

Trixie's necklace was made of a material of unknown origin. Could there still be elements man didn't know about in this day and age?

And what about that project Professor Aaron was working on in New Mexico just before his disappearance? Was his translation of an ancient American Indian language related to his disappearance, or even the death of his daughter's husband, Henri? And how was all this tied to the kidnapping of Mariah's children? Most importantly, why was Keenan Darstow involved, so much so that he would actually kidnap children to achieve his mysterious ends?

His mind was crowded with questions, and he had precious few answers. He would send Trixie to see Mariah. Meanwhile, he would try to connect up with Thomas and the boy. Maybe Thomas and Mariah Bourassa would have new information that would shed some light on this mess.

CHAPTER TWENTY-FIVE

Low Earth Orbit

It had been a thrill each time Marcus had done it. He remembered that first time, when desperate to go before being discovered, he had sat before the panel, drawn a deep breath, and pressed what he had only surmised was the correct icon sequence.

At first, he had noticed only a high-pitched whine, like the sound a computer processor makes when first turned on. And then, as if by magic, the solid metal wall opposite him became transparent, allowing him to see everything outside the shuttle. Slowly, the shuttle had risen a few feet off the ground, and then stopped. And then, without warning, it had maneuvered out of the hanger bay, assumed a forty-five degree pitch, and shot into the eastern sky at an incredible rate of climb.

He had passed out that first trip. But now, having mastered the controls and having become accustomed to accelerated G forces, he was able to remain conscious during flights. It didn't really matter if he passed out, though. The shuttle always returned to the Mother Ship if his hands left the control panel.

What he enjoyed most was the sensation of gliding merely a few hundred feet over the ground. It was as smooth, airy, and quiet as if he was on a magic carpet. Except this was far more than just a unique aircraft. It was the key out of the known.

He would not act precipitously. He would only meet her if it was safe, and in circumstances where she had sufficient time to choose.

He had done what he could for the oppressed in Asia. And in doing so, he had learned the quirks of the shuttle's visible spectrum weapons systems. Now it was time to see if those systems or the other amazing systems on board would make the difference between success or failure in his quest to see his daughter and grandchildren one last time.

Marcus caressed the now familiar control panel, festooned with words he alone could understand. It was time. He set the coordinates, and maneuvered the shuttle away from the loading bay. Below him revolved the brilliant blue planet that soon, he would no longer call home.

CHAPTER TWENTY-SIX

Medicine Stone Lake, New Mexico

It had taken them until dawn to make the lake, and Thomas had trouble staying awake the past half hour. Still, he pushed on, knowing any delay might seal their fate.

The fragrant, pine-scented air had become noticeably colder. Below them and to the left, as they glided up the twisted dirt road leading to Old Vic's, lay the lapis depths of Medicine Stone Lake, where Thomas often fished in his youth.

The lodge was unchanged since he had seen it last, over ten years ago. There was no sign of anyone about, but Thomas didn't call out a greeting. Instead, he pulled the bike up to the log barn and ordered Jacob to dismount. It was only then that he discovered the boy was asleep, his tiny hands tightly gripped to the back of Thomas's jacket. As gently as possible, so as not to startle the boy, Thomas roused him and lifted him to the ground. Thomas then dismounted, gripped the boy's hand, and led him around the back of the lodge. As he expected, the rear door, which led into a large, screened porch facing the lake, was unlocked.

"Stay here," Thomas directed the boy. Jacob nodded, looking longingly at a battered, overstuffed couch at the west wall of the porch.

Thomas crept into the lodge and closed the door separating the porch from the building's great room. He kept close to the north wall, listening for any sign that the lodge was inhabited.

Occasionally, a board underfoot would send out an obscene creak, and Thomas cursed himself for moving too quickly.

The door to Old Vic's bedroom was closed, as it should be this time of day. Sleep was sacred to the old man, as sacred as his penchant for drinking beer with breakfast and drowning his pancakes with catsup. But disturbing Old Vic's sleep had more dire consequences than merely arousing his ire. There was Waldo to contend with. All 1,400 pounds of him, not to mention his eleven-inch claws.

It had been many years since he had been around Waldo, and Thomas was certain the grizzly would not recognize him as a friend. That meant the bear would attack the instant it sensed Thomas, unless Old Vic had the presence of mind to call him off.

The bear always slept at the foot of Old Vic's bed whenever his master was resting. During Thomas's first summer at the lake, a drunken Swede named Nils Anderson had broken into the lodge to steal whatever he could carry off. Hearing Anderson rifle through a large dresser flanking the west wall of the lodge's great room, Waldo had broken through the huge wooden door separating Old Vic's bedroom from the great room and ripped off both of Anderson's arms before Old Vic could stop him. Anderson only lived because he was so drunk he didn't go into shock.

Of course, if such a thing had happened in the city, there would have been a great hue and cry to euthanize the bear, and no doubt, Anderson would have been besieged by lawyers urging him to sue Old Vic for allowing such a dangerous animal to attack a petty thief. But perspectives were a bit different in the country, and most folks around thought that Anderson got what he had deserved.

Thomas crept past the bedroom and into the narrow kitchen adjoining it. The old propane powered refrigerators stood there, each flanking one side of the ancient wood stove Vic used to prepare all of his meals. Using all the care he could muster, Thomas quietly lifted the latch on the left refrigerator and slowly opened the door. Sure enough, the fridge was stocked to the gills with leftovers, which the old man called 'Dejafood,' and Stroh's long-necks. Trying not to make any noise, he gathered up four beers and crept back to Vic's bedroom. Behind the door, he heard Waldo snoring heavily.

The floor of Old Vic's bedroom was two inches below the level of the great room's floor. Reaching into his pocket, Thomas extracted a *Swiss Army* knife and used the bottle opener to uncap each beer. He slowly poured the beers under the door, stepped back, and waited.

Waldo's snoring suddenly stopped. Within a few moments, Thomas heard the bear lapping up the beer. He used the opportunity to creep back into the kitchen and gather up another four beers to repeat the ritual. Waldo seemed to lap the beer up from under the door almost as fast as Thomas could pour it.

After making two more trips to the refrigerator, Thomas noticed that the beer poured under the door was not disappearing as fast as before. He heard a tremendous thud, as the bear fell to the floor in a stupor. Thomas wiped his brow with relief. It was then that he felt the shot of hot breath on his neck.

CHAPTER TWENTY-SEVEN

Santa Fe, New Mexico

They had taken adjoining rooms at the Santa Fe Hilton. Trixie, as she insisted he call her, had taken a cab to Mariah Bourassa's, leaving Dov with the rental car, a tiny Geo Prism. The crisp air was tinged with the scent of burned mesquite. Dov drew in a deep breath before squeezing into the Prism for the drive to Thomas Kuzmic's home.

Being an ancient city, Santa Fe is not laid out in the most logical of fashions, and it took Dov some time to locate Kuzmic's address on his fold-out map of the city. The house was on the outskirts of town, adjoining a vast expanse of forested, hilly terrain. Dov could see how Thomas was attracted to the place. The surrounding forest had an almost mystical aura.

Dov parked in the carport and sensed trouble the instant he reached the door. Both panes of the divided front window had been pierced by some sort of ordinance -- perhaps tear gas rounds. The front door was ajar, and spent nine-millimeter casings covered the entry hall. From the number of casings present, Dov surmised that they had been ejected by automatic weapons.

Dov drew his service weapon, a SIG-Sauer nine-millimeter holding fifteen rounds, and slowly crept through the first and second floors of the house. It appeared he was alone.

Evidently, there had been one hell of a battle, although he saw no blood splatter patterns or evidence that anyone had been injured. Thomas's pet pigeon lay dead in its cage, possibly poisoned by exposure to tear gas. Many of the rooms were in shambles, with Thomas's effects yanked from drawers and shelves and tossed to the floor.

He would have missed the stairs leading to the basement if he hadn't nearly slipped on a spent shell casing in front of the door that separated the stairs from the kitchen. As soon as he opened the door, his nostrils were stung by the acrid smell of cordite.

The light bulbs leading down the staircase had been broken out. Dov searched the house for a flashlight. Finding one in the kitchen, he flicked it on and cautiously proceeded down the darkened stairs. Bullet casings lay everywhere.

A steel safe house? Thomas always talked about how everyone should have such a thing, but Dov had always thought he had been kidding. The expense to install the safe must have been enormous. He hoped it had been justified. The heavy door to the safe had been blown off. It must have taken more than several charges, because the door's entire length had been pasted with separate blast marks.

The safe was large enough for three or four people to sit in. The cabinets that lined its walls were nearly empty -- all that remained in the safe were a few granola bars and some first-aid equipment. Directly opposite the safe door, in its interior, was what appeared to be a steel plate, with a large, jagged hole punched through its center. Gingerly, Thomas slipped through into something from an *Indiana Jones* movie.

As he crept down the mine passage, Dov occasionally looked over his shoulder, half expecting to see a monumental boulder bearing down on him as in *Raiders of the Lost Arc*.

From the many tracks at the mouth of the passage, it seemed as if a motorcycle of some kind had sped out to the street into which the passage had emptied. The footprints of several booted men were clear as well as...a small print -- that of a boy.

Not wishing to trudge back up the mine passage, Dov walked out into the street and found his way back to Thomas's house through the neighborhood.

Medicine Stone Lake, Thomas had told him. Dov spread his fold-out map of New Mexico onto the hood of the Geo Prism. *Where the heck was Medicine Stone?*

He was completely unaware of the scarlet laser-beam centered directly on his forehead.

CHAPTER TWENTY-EIGHT

Santa Fe, New Mexico

She was surprised when a man identifying himself as an FBI agent opened the door.

"May I help you, ma'am?" Agent Leland inquired.

"Well, ah yes. I'm Dr. Beatrice Pentov. Ms. Bourassa is expecting me?"

Leland said, "Please, wait a moment, will you?" He closed the door, leaving Trixie on the steps. A few minutes later, the door burst open and Mariah strongly embraced her.

"I'm so glad you could come."

"Well, my dear, it is my pleasure." Trixie handed Mariah a gift-wrapped box. "A small present."

Suddenly, Leland stepped forward, reaching for the box. Mariah snatched it away, simultaneously glaring at Leland. "This is a gift for me, Agent Leland. Please leave us alone."

Leland hesitated for a moment, and then retreated into the house.

Mariah took Trixie's hand, and led her onto the sidewalk. "Take a walk with me?"

"Sure. I could use the exercise after the flight."

They walked for a while in silence. "How are Jacob and Brittany?"

Mariah's face grew taut, and she nearly began to cry.

"My children have been kidnapped!" she whispered. "It has something to do with the Professor's disappearance." Quietly, she related all she knew, including her father's holographic message. Trixie listened in silence.

Mariah looked directly into Trixie's eyes.

"Did you bring the gift mentioned in the holograph?"

"Your holding it, dear. It's in the box."

Mariah resisted the urge to tear off the wrapper. "I'm sure they are watching us, perhaps trying to listen to us," she said. "I'll open it in the bathroom when we get inside. What is it?"

"You'll see soon enough," Trixie replied. "But I have to say, I'm not sure how it will unite you with either your father or your children."

CHAPTER TWENTY-NINE

Roswell, New Mexico

Andrew felt awfully conspicuous. He stood outside *The Little Green Men*, whose sign declared the name of the establishment in ugly block letters traced in green neon piping. As he passed across the threshold, he felt a bit like the famed Wyatt Earp entering the apocryphal saloon.

No one seemed to notice his entrance, and he bellied up to the bar, which was attended by a middle-aged woman whose aquamarine blouse was rolled up to reveal several tattoos on each forearm. She had rings on all her fingers, and her skin was almost as wrinkled as that of a crocodile. She ignored Andrew completely.

To his right, several booths overflowed with what appeared to be cowboys and rather unsavory looking women. To his immediate left several other cowboys leaned over their drinks, watching an extraordinary program concerning men who rode bulls in a ring. The decor appeared to be an ungodly hybrid of cowboy and science fiction themes. Andrew was instantly fascinated.

"Say there, madam," he bellowed to the barmaid. She ignored him. After unsuccessfully trying to draw her attention with hand gestures, Andrew left the bar and walked up to a table where an elderly man with a dirty straw hat nursed a pint.

He thrust his hand toward the man, and said, "Good evening sir. I'm Andrew Sawyer, from London."

A bit startled, the man smiled.

"Yer not from around these parts then, eh?"

"No, London, England -- Great Britain?"

The man thought a moment. "I thought you was a ferner 'cause a yer accent."

"Yes, well, believe it or not, I've come all the way from England just to visit this bar."

At that, the barmaid turned toward Andrew.

"You gotta be kidding."

"I assure you madam, I am not."

The woman screwed up her face. "Why the hell would anyone cross an ocean and most of the states just to come to this hell hole?"

"Madam, may I speak frankly?" Andrew's sincerity had piqued her curiosity, as well as that of the surrounding patrons.

"Absolutely, buster. Why, you can speak any damn way you please in here."

"Well, I'm a reporter for one of London's most prestigious papers," he exaggerated. "And I am researching a story about certain secret weapons being used by the American government." He paused to see if all this had an effect on his audience, but he couldn't discern anything from their weathered faces.

"Well anyway, we believe these weapons are space-based lasers, probably positioned on orbiting satellites, which have the ability to blind pilots and ground troops anywhere in the world. And believe it or not, we've had a lead that someone around here has some knowledge about these weapons."

"Say what?" the bartender responded.

"Well, I never heard a such thangs," his companion said, as he scratched his head. "But, maybe some o' the boys at the base know something."

"What base?" Andrew asked.

"Why, the air force base just west of town, near Socorro," the barmaid added. "Surely, as a reporter, you would a knowd that?"

Andrew blushed. He had not taken time to do anything but speed to the bar in as little time as possible. He knew nothing of New Mexico other than what he had read on the face of the state map he had purchased at the car rental agency in Albuquerque.

"Could I have a beer, madam?"

The barmaid scowled, but drew him a draft.

"On the house, Mr. Reporter," she cackled. "In the interest o' diplomatic relations."

Andrew turned toward his companion.

"What do they do over at the base?"

The man again thought for a while before he spoke. "Well, if you weren't a Britisher, I wouldn't tell ya because ya could be a spy. But I s'pose yer okay since we're friends with the British."

Andrew nodded seriously.

"Well, as far as I kin tell," the man said, "they just fly helicopters in and fly 'em out, and in between those times, they dig darned near the biggest holes I ever seen, and then cover 'em up with buildings."

"Why do they dig the holes?" Andrew asked.

"Don't know. Maybe cause they want basements to their buildings. Or maybe just to waste taxpayer money cause they have to spend it before year end or they don't git more for the next year."

Men in the bar chuckled and nudged one another.

Andrew searched for a way out of the conversation, "This establishment's got a funny name. How did it come to be called *The Little Green Men?*"

His companion's face lit up. "Why shit, you really don't know damn about Roswell, do you?"

Andrew felt the fool. He felt even more foolish since he was being embarrassed by an imbecile.

"I'm sorry. I really don't."

"July 2, 1947." The man winked. "Everything's on file at the library. It'll be open tomorrow morning, and you can read all about it."

Andrew said he would.

"And then you can come see me." The man wrote a telephone number on a beer-soaked napkin and pushed it into Andrew's hand. "I was only eight at the time, but my Pa saw everythin', and he told me everythin' he saw." With that, the man got up and left, waving to the barmaid as he stumbled out the door.

Andrew put five dollars on the bar and followed the man out, but could not find him. He glanced about, searching for lodging. He spied a dilapidated sign battered by the wind that read, "Slipper Inn Motel."

Surely, it had to be better than his accommodations in Nepal.

CHAPTER THIRTY

Medicine Stone Lake, New Mexico

For one of the few times in his life, Thomas was terrified. There, standing before him on his hind quarters, Waldo appeared even larger than Thomas had remembered. Thomas screamed and ran toward the back porch as fast as he could, with Waldo trotting not far behind. Thomas slammed the flimsy door that separated the great room from the back porch, grabbed the sleeping Jacob by the torso and ran as fast as possible down the cedar-wood deck to the boathouse.

"Christ, no boat." Thomas panted. "Can you swim kid?"

Jolted awake, Jacob nodded, and with that, Thomas gripped the boy tightly and dove off the boathouse dock, which was nearly three feet above the waterline.

While all bears swim, few enjoy it, and all dislike heights. As Thomas had hoped, the bear declined to follow them into the water, choosing instead to sniff the site where they had launched themselves off the dock. He then bellowed and roared, causing the waterfowl around the lake to leave their perches and scatter in all directions.

"I'm sinking." Jacob cried. Thomas gathered him up and managed to sidestroke out about twenty-five yards from the dock.

What the hell do we do now?

"Goddamn it. That you, Tommy?" Thomas turned. There to his right was Old Vic, standing in a rowboat wearing a sweat stained T-shirt and boxer shorts. The boat was powered by an electric outboard, whose quiet operation had masked Old Vic's approach.

"Heck yes you old bastard. Take the kid." With that, Thomas passed Jacob up to the lean old man, who dragged the boy over the gunnels into the boat's mid-section. "You'll tip the boat Tommy -- just swim to the dock, and I'll call off Boris."

"That's not Waldo?"

"Waldo? You got Waldo all snookered. That's how's I knew it was you, cause nobody else knows how much that bear likes beer."

"Well, when did you get Boris?"

"You just come in and dry off. I'll give you the lowdown then." With that, Vic turned the boat and sped toward shore.

Thomas treaded water while Vic introduced Jacob to Boris, the bear, and then returned with the bear and boy to the lodge. Thomas swam back to the dock and climbed up the two-by-four ladder placed at the far east end of the boathouse. He slowly walked up the dock ready, at the first sign of Boris, to turn and run.

"Hurry up and come inside, you wimp," Vic yelled. Thomas quickened his pace and walked onto the porch. There was Old Vic and Boris, who Jacob was now petting as if he was the household retriever.

"How did you come by Boris?" Thomas asked.

"Travlin' circus -- Soviets, in fact. They were puttin' on quite a show in Roswell when the Commie government fell a few years back. Well, most of the performers just quit the circus and took off for parts unknown, leaving Boris here, and a bunch of other animals without a home. Boris is a she, by the way, and that's why the two bears get along so well. In any event, somebody told Game and Fish about Waldo, and they asked if I would care for Boris until they found a home for her. I guess they just plumb forgot about her, cause I've had 'er ever since."

"Is she as ornery as Waldo?"

"Sometimes, especially with strangers. She'll give you quite a chase if you run from her like you did, or bother me, of course."

"Does she ever fight with Waldo?"

"They take nips out of each other, every so often, but I think they do okay. Cost me a fortune to feed 'em, though."

"I bet," Thomas muttered as he pulled off his soaked shirt and pants and left them in a pile on the porch steps.

"And who's this?" Vic asked, looking at Jacob.

"It's a long story," Thomas said as he walked through the porch to hunt up some clothes.

"Always is with you, boy," Vic sighed. He took Jacob by the hand, and together they followed Thomas inside. Boris stayed on the porch, amusing himself by tearing Thomas's shirt to shreds.

CHAPTER THIRTY-ONE

Santa Fe, New Mexico

Mariah sat on the toilet lid, with Trixie perched on the flat edge of the bathtub. They spoke in whispers, even though the bathroom door was closed. "Go ahead and open it," Trixie whispered.

Mariah gingerly removed the gift wrap and slipped her nail between the edges of the box bound by tape. Inside lay the turquoise necklace. She took in a sharp breath, smiling, "It's incredibly beautiful."

"I thought so, too. Put it on."

Mariah draped the necklace around her neck, arranging its pendent between her full, uplifted breasts. She looked at Trixie for approval.

"It's you," Trixie said. "But now what?"

"I don't know." Mariah took it off and handed it back to Trixie. "Here, you keep it. Dad gave it to you."

"No dear. His message to you said that I was to bring it to you, and anyway, it looks far better on you than me." Trixie pushed it back into Mariah's hands. "Please keep it."

Mariah smiled and reached forward to hug Trixie. "I'm ashamed about the way I felt about you all these years. I perceived you as my mother's rival, even after she died."

They embraced.

"Well, how about some lunch?" Trixie asked.

Mariah didn't respond.

"Dear?"

Mariah was looking at her right hand, which had been tightly grasping the necklace. An incredible light emanated from the necklace, so bright that she could see through her hand as if it was a colored X-ray. Frightened, she dropped the necklace in the bathtub, where it immediately darkened back to its normal appearance.

"Did you…did you see that?" Mariah gasped, shaking.

"The light?" Trixie asked.

Mariah picked up the necklace again and held it tightly. "It lit up when I gripped it," she said. Nothing happened, and after repeating the procedure several times, she let the necklace slip to the floor and cried.

"Damn it, what am I doing wrong?" she sobbed. Trixie picked up the necklace and examined it closely.

"What is Tuzigoot 911?" She pointed to the face of the turquoise pendant, which had cleared to reveal the name and numbers in smoky white letters.

Mariah grabbed the necklace. "I don't know what it is. It must be the message he wanted me to have. Is Tuzigoot an Indian word?"

Trixie thought a moment. "Probably. Although I don't recognize it. I think we should assume it is, perhaps from an ancient American tribe your father was studying, like the Anasazi or Hohokom. I'll do some research locally, and see if I can come up with an answer." She rose to leave.

Mariah grasped Trixie by the shoulders and drew her away from the door. "Please don't tell anyone about this." She searched Trixie's eyes for compliance.

"I'll tell no one dear, unless you say otherwise."

Mariah brightened and opened the door. There, taking up the entire doorframe, was Keenan Darstow.

CHAPTER THIRTY-TWO

Roswell, New Mexico

His first instinct was to skip the library altogether and investigate the nearby air force base. But something about the decrepit rancher's tone of voice, and the fact he referenced a specific date long since past, persuaded Andrew to check out the date referenced.

The library had placed all newspaper accounts prior to 1980 on microfiche. Andrew had requested the microfiche disc for the summer of 1947, and he was steadily progressing through the pages of the *Roswell Telegraph* in search of the issue beginning July 2nd of that year.

Andrew felt a tinge of excitement. Nothing on the front page, except pieces on the local high school American football team, a new model Chevrolet being displayed in a local dealership, and some thieves caught stealing cattle from a rancher. Andrew slowly paged through the paper, looking for something extraordinary, although he hadn't any thoughts as to what. To his dismay, he found nothing of note, and so he went on to the next day's issue. He found what he was looking for on the front page, below the crease. "Flying Saucer Flies Over Town," read the small headline.

"Numerous residents telephoned the Sheriff's office last night, claiming to see a flying saucer, measuring twenty to thirty feet in diameter, pass over town. All who reported the sighting claimed the saucer appeared to have stability problems, and one person, Mrs. Hazel Meorga, claimed to see the saucer crash out toward the direction of William (Mac) Brazel's ranch. Contacted by the *Telegraph* late last night, Mr. Brazel said he did hear what he thought was a tremendous explosion about eight o'clock in the evening, but he was sure it was nothing more than a thunderclap, since it had been raining heavily since early afternoon.

"Sheriff Charles Herzog said he had no evidence proving the reports. Apparently, the Sheriff's office intends to take no action at this time."

Nothing further about the incident was in the July 3rd issue, and Andrew began thumbing through the July 4th issue. Apparently, July 4th was a national holiday celebrating the colonies' independence from the crown, and most of the stories on the front page were devoted to this theme.

On the third page, under "Local News," he found another story related to the saucer reported on July 3rd.

"Strange Metal Found at Brazel's Ranch," the small headline read:

"Rancher William (Mac) Brazel has reported numerous pieces of strange metal strewn all about his east pasture. Some of the metal looked like large beams, about four to five feet long and about a half foot in width. The beams appeared to be covered with strange hieroglyphics and were as light as balsa wood, but extremely strong.

"Mr. Brazel collected as much of the metal as he could find and is storing it in his barn. Anyone knowing where the metal came from or who owns it is asked to inquire at the Brazel Ranch or contact Sheriff Herzog, who in turn, has notified Roswell Army Air Field in case the metal is debris from one of their balloons or planes."

He read on, frantically searching for another story about the saucer or the strange debris. No stories about either appeared for several days. Then, the following story appeared on the front page of the July 7th issue:

"Wreckage of Flying Disc Found

"Major Jesse Marcel, an intelligence officer attached to Roswell Army Air Field, issued a statement this morning confirming that the wreckage of a flying disc of unknown origin had been recovered at William (Mac) Brazel's Ranch. According to Major Marcel, the wreckage was comprised of strange, lightweight metal that appeared to be virtually indestructible. Major Marcel said he was not able to dent the metal with a sledgehammer, nor was he able to burn or melt it. Further, the metal was extremely flexible, and seemed to have a "memory"; when folded, it would unfold itself, leaving no creases.

"Pursuant to the orders of Colonel William Blanchard, commander of Roswell Army Air Field, all traces of the metal recovered are to be transported to Carswell Air Force Base in Fort Worth, Texas, for further testing. Major Marcel denied that any aliens, living or dead were found in the wreckage."

Nothing further about the metal recovered at Brazel's Ranch was reported for about a week. Then, the following story appeared in the Sunday, July 15th, issue of the *Telegraph*, in the "Local News" section:

"Student Claims to Find Dead Aliens in Desert

"A University of New Mexico student, Grady L. Barnett, reported Saturday that while hiking, he found a flying saucer that had apparently crashed in the desert near Magdalena, a small village just west of Socorro, New Mexico. Mr. Barnett says that the craft appeared to be about thirty feet in diameter, and was essentially intact. Adjacent to the saucer were what appeared to be three aliens, who appeared to be dead. Barnett described them as short but humanoid in form and dressed in metallic, one-piece suits without zippers or buttons. The aliens' heads were rounder than normal, with small eyes and no hair.

"Mr. Barnett reported that shortly after he began inspecting the saucer and alien bodies, a small group of scientists from the University of Pennsylvania arrived, who began their own investigation. About an hour later, officers from Roswell Army Air Field arrived and escorted Mr. Barnett off site.

"Representatives of the University of Pennsylvania confirm that they had an archec logical research team operating at an Anasazi dig near Magdalena, but deny that the team saw any flying saucers or alien bodies. Lieutenant William Haut, Press Liaison for Roswell Army Air Field, would only confirm that Mr. Barnett had stumbled across some metallic debris. When asked about Mr. Barnett's claims concerning alien bodies, Lieutenant Haut replied, "Who are you going to believe, the U.S. Army, or some sun-stroked student?"

"The *Telegraph* was unable to view the site described by Mr. Barnett, since the army has cordoned off the area. Lieutenant Haut emphasized that the area will be reopened when all of the debris is recovered."

Andrew only found one other reference to the saucers or aliens, other than a host of excited, sometimes hysterical letters to the editor concerning an anticipated alien invasion. The last story read:

"Flying Saucers Really Balloons, Says Army

Lieutenant William Haut, Press Liaison for Roswell Army Air Field, issued a press release this afternoon which said that the debris scattered about William (Mac) Brazel's Ranch and reported to have been seen near Magdalena by University of New Mexico student, Grady L. Barnett, was really the remains of an experimental balloon outfitted with a "state of the art radar reflecting dish" made of new metals created through advanced atomic technology. Lieutenant

Haut stated that earlier reports by Major Marcel that the metal recovered was of unknown origin had been erroneous. Major Marcel had simply been unaware that the metal comprising the balloon was of a new type created by army scientists. Further, Major Marcel's earlier comment that the metal was the debris of a flying disc of unknown origin was erroneous, as well. Major Marcel had been unaware of the balloon's mission, and like some Roswell citizens, had 'jumped to unwarranted conclusions.' Lieutenant Haut apologized for any discomfort or anxiety caused by Major Marcel's earlier comments."

After paging through several more weeks of the *Telegraph*, Andrew saw no further references to the saucer/alien stories. However, three weeks after Lieutenant Haut's last press release, a small item appeared in the "Events About Town" section of the *Telegraph*:

"Government to Build Small Facility Near Magdalena

"The federal government announced that it intends to build a small research facility on the outskirts of Socorro, near the small village of Magdalena. The facility will house thirty to forty scientists, who intend to study Anasazi ruins recently uncovered just outside Magdalena. Due to the fragile nature of the ruins, only persons cleared by the government will be allowed onto the facility or near the ruins. Nevertheless, the residents of Socorro and Magdalena hope the facility will bring much needed revenue to their merchants."

Andrew rose from his chair. Who are they kidding? Could the Magdalena facility still exist?

CHAPTER THIRTY-THREE

Santa Fe, New Mexico

Trixie had never been so startled. They both screamed when Mariah opened the bathroom door to reveal Agent Darstow towering over them. Mariah fainted onto the carpet in a heap. As she fell, the pendant slipped from her right hand. Darstow quickly retrieved it, stuffed it into his pocket as he lifted Mariah to the bed, and directed the other agent to fetch some water.

Trixie had been too unnerved to ask for the pendant to be returned. Perhaps if she had done so, it would have drawn unnecessary attention to the necklace. On the other hand, one glance at the face of the pendant might reveal the message apparently only destined for Mariah's eyes. Trixie felt so helpless.

The agents urged her to leave, assuring her that they would summon medical attention, if necessary. And so, with great misgivings, she taxied back to metro Santa Fe, with more questions than answers.

Trixie arrived at the Hilton's parking lot at dusk. She showered and changed into a long maroon and black-patterned skirt and cream-colored blouse for her seven o'clock meeting with Dov at the hotel's restaurant. She decided to tell Dov everything but the pendant's message; after all, that was the only secret Mariah urged her to keep.

Dov was at a table by the time she arrived at the restaurant. He stood as she slipped to her chair.

"Please, Dov, don't be so formal."

"I always rise when a beautiful woman is seated."

Trixie flushed, and arranged her napkin. After the waiter got their drink orders, Dov cleared his throat.

"I need your help." He bit his lip for a moment. "I'm going to confide all I know to you, even though that violates Bureau policy and the Official Secrets Act."

Trixie looked at him expectantly. In hushed tones, Dov related all he had learned about the Bourassas and Marcus Aaron. He then described Jacob Bourassa's escape from the safe house, as well as his supposition that Jacob and Thomas had fled Thomas's home after being closely pursued by Darstow's men.

"So you believe that one of your own agents-- this Darstow-- may have actually staged the kidnapping of Mariah's children?" Trixie asked.

"I know that sounds bizarre, but it's a strong possibility. As to why, I don't know, except to say that it may have something to do with what Mariah's father or husband were working on at the time the husband was killed and her father disappeared."

Trixie winced. "I too am going to confide in you, Dov. But in doing so, I am revealing a secret that only this afternoon I had promised to keep inviolate. I want you to realize that I'm only confiding in you because I truly believe you can help Mariah. It is not my practice to break my word."

Dov nodded solemnly, and Trixie related all that she could recall from her afternoon encounter with Mariah, including the strange message emanating from the pendant.

"Do you have any idea what 'Tuzigoot 911' means?"

"No, although Tuzigoot sounds American Indian. And 911 could mean 'emergency' or even 'September 11,' just two days from now."

Dov looked earnestly into Trixie's eyes. "The 911 designation could mean both 'emergency' and 'September 11.'"

"If that's the case," Trixie cautioned, "we better find out what 'Tuzigoot' means."

CHAPTER THIRTY-FOUR

Magdalena, New Mexico

Couldn't just once I find a lead that wasn't down a dusty, dirt road?

Apparently, all roads to Magdalena were unpaved, and to make matters worse, few of the roads had signs. As a result, Andrew had gotten himself lost a half dozen times until finally stumbling onto a shepherd that, in broken English, had set him onto the proper course.

Magdalena was little more than a few storefronts surrounded by double the amount of taverns. The shepherd had told him that the government archeology facility was still inhabited, and was located at the far end of the village in a valley surrounded by Joshua trees. He hoped to see it as he wound his way through the village.

He thought it would look like the classic archeology site, low mud foundations swarming with archeologists on bent knees earnestly digging with trowels for lost treasures. Instead, the facility looked very much like a small air force base, with several two-story warehouse-type buildings without any windows ringed by a high chain-link fence topped with barbed and razor wire. At the rear of the facility there was a large helicopter landing pad, and the only entrance appeared to be a gate manned by two solemn-looking sentries armed with side-arms and machine guns.

Andrew drove up to the gate and handed one of the sentries his press credentials. "Andrew Sawyer, sir, from London, to see your press attaché?"

The guard frowned at Andrew and asked, "Do you have an appointment?"

"Well, no, but I would very much like to speak with the base press liaison or attaché."

The guard slipped into the sentry post and lifted a telephone receiver. After speaking for several seconds, he set the receiver down and returned with a pencil and pad of paper.

"Please write down your name and where you are staying locally. The Commander will contact you and arrange for a tour."

It was very apparent this was as far as Andrew was going to get at this point, so he jotted down his name, as well as that of his motel, the "Slipper Inn." This was one occasion he wished he had checked into a finer establishment.

The sentry chuckled at the name of Andrew's motel.

"It was all that was available when I arrived," Andrew explained.

The guard waved him goodbye, and he backed the car out of the gate to return to Roswell. Andrew leaned out his window. "Could you give me directions on the shortest route to Roswell?"

The guard described a route completely different than that he had taken, and he set off, certain he had taken down the guard's directions correctly.

After several hours, he became completely lost in a vast wilderness of twisted juniper bushes and prickly pear cactus. To make matters worse, he had run out of petrol, and there wasn't a filling station in sight. Always stay with your car when stranded, Andrew remembered reading. And so he did, often napping in the back seat as the day turned to dusk and then the blackest of nights.

It became quite cold in the car, and Andrew rolled up the windows to prevent any more cold air from getting in. A thin film of moisture covered the windows, making them opaque.

Suddenly, a flash of light fell upon the windshield. Must be a car heading up the road in my direction, Andrew surmised. He bolted out of the car, hoping to wave down the oncoming car. But there was no car. There was nothing, as far as he could see. Nothing except every hair on his entire body stood straight up.

CHAPTER THIRTY-FIVE

Santa Fe, New Mexico

"I had 'em in my laser sights as soon as he left the cave," Mentol bragged.

"So, Bar-Lev is on to us." Darstow looked across the room at Mentol, who himself was staring out the dirty window of the factory floor where they were keeping Brittany Bourassa. "What to do now?"

"Get the Director to order him off," Mentol offered. "Surely, he'll have to withdraw?"

Darstow said nothing, and drummed his fingers on the wooden bench he leaned on. "The Director doesn't know about our little charade. All he knows is that the ship is missing. While he has authorized all means to retrieve it, I suspect he might frown on kidnapping."

"Take Bar-Lev into yer confidence; maybe he'll agree to play along."

Darstow snorted. "No way. The man's a Boy Scout. He'll blow the entire operation."

Darstow stood and paced to the opposite wall, which was strewn with graffiti. "Do nothing for the moment. Let's see if our Jew Assistant Director can lead us to Kuzmic and the boy. If we're lucky, Mr. Mentol, you and your team may get to have your way with the lot."

CHAPTER THIRTY-SIX

Medicine Stone Lake, New Mexico

They agreed that Dov would try to reconnect with Thomas Kuzmic at Medicine Stone Lake while Trixie stayed in Santa Fe to research the significance of Tuzigoot. Dov was to return to town by the evening of September 10th, which would leave them twenty-four hours to go to or get Tuzigoot, wherever that was or might be. It had taken Dov half the morning to find a map detailed enough to pinpoint the lake's location, and he drove nearly four hours to get there. He was amazed how cool it had become the last mile leading up to the lake. The car's heater wouldn't work, so he fastened the top button of his tweed blazer, and wished he had thought to bring some gloves.

Luckily, there appeared to only be one road leading to the lake from the main highway, and Dov bounced down it without incident. After driving nearly all the way around the lake's circumference, he came to a large log-lodge flanked by a similarly constructed barn and several other log buildings. Immediately behind the lodge lay the blue expanse of Medicine Stone, which shined like a mirror in the afternoon light.

Dov got out of the little Prism and glanced around. No one else was about. This appeared to be the only house on the lake, so he was hopeful this was the legendary Old Vic's, where Thomas had spent most of his youth. There was something Thomas had told him about the place that Dov couldn't quite remember. Something remarkable. Damn, he couldn't quite put his finger on it.

There was no doorbell or buzzer. Gingerly, he knocked on the front door. When he received no answer, he knocked harder, putting his ear to the door in hopes of hearing some activity inside. He heard nothing, although a foul odor seemed to seep from under the door.

The smell was similar to that of decaying flesh. Dov tried the doorknob. It was unlocked. Slowly, he opened the door. Something was blocking the door from opening all the way. He pushed the door forcefully and heard a sort of low bellow. He stepped back, and out the door shot the largest grizzly bear Dov had ever seen.

Hastened more by terror than design, Dov leaped back from the door and bolted to the Prism, which, in accord with his habit, he had locked. The bear padded out the door after him. Dov was so frightened, his shaking hands prevented him from fitting the key into the door lock. Not knowing what else to do, Dov ran to the barn door, hoping it was unlocked. No more than ten feet separated Dov from his pursuer.

There was a two-foot gap in the barn door, and Dov dove inside, desperately grasping for some handhold in which to drive the door shut. Not finding anything, he dug his nails into the door's timbers and with all his strength, multiplied by the gallons of adrenaline being fed by his pituitary, slammed the door closed on the bear's snout. The bear let out a terrifying howl, and then raked the door with his claws. He then withdrew to the center of the driveway, laying down on all fours facing the barn door. Dov could see him clearly from a dirty window set in the barn's front wall.

He was soaked in sweat, and hyperventilated so much he feared passing out. He searched for a back entrance, but found none. He would just have to wait until the bear wondered off.

Singing? He thought he heard someone singing. Dov spit on the dirty windowpane to get a better view of the drive. There was someone coming up the drive from the back of the lodge. It looked like a small boy, dark brown hair, about eight years old. Did he see the bear? What if the bear turned on him?

The boy kept walking toward the bear. Remarkably, although the bear must have seen the boy, it paid no attention to him. Instead, it kept its eyes centered on the barn door, where Dov had retreated.

Dov felt he had to warn the boy off from the bear. Perhaps he didn't realize the danger the grizzly posed. Using his gun, he broke out a portion of the windowpane, yelling, "Hey, get away from that bear. He could hurt you."

The boy stopped in his tracks, searching for the location of Dov's cries.

"Here, in the barn. I ran in here to get away from the bear. Go back into the lodge and get help."

The boy ran to the lodge. The bear completely ignored him and continued to focus on the barn door and Dov.

After a few minutes, a second bear padded up the drive. This one was slightly smaller than the first. It slapped the first bear on the left side with its front paw, but got little reaction. The second bear then drew alongside the first bear and lay down on its massive haunches. Great, now he was dinner for two bears.

"What took you so long?"

Dov jerked around just as Thomas de-cocked his pistol, which, he surmised, had been leveled at his back.

Relieved at finding Thomas, but embarrassed at being out maneuvered, Dov sputtered, "How, how did you get in? I couldn't find any back exit."

Thomas laughed and pointed towards the rear wall. "There's a hole in the wall behind that old set of milk crates. We used to sneak in that way to smoke." They embraced, but Thomas drew away quickly, wiping his hands on his jeans. "You're as wet as a seal."

"Those bears scared the crap out of me. My heart's still pounding. Do you still have the boy?"

"You saw him. We had just come back off the lake from fishing, and when he spied you, he thought you were one of Darstow's men."

"I've got a lot to tell you. Let's get out of here." Dov got down on his hands and knees, preparing to crawl out the hidden exit. Thomas grabbed him by the arm and pulled him up. He then walked up to the barn's front door and slid it open.

"Are you crazy?" Dov frantically glanced around for a place to hide. Finding none, he drew and chambered a round in his gun, hoping to scare the bears off should they attack.

Thomas laughed and without a glance towards Dov, walked out of the barn right up to the bears, who stood up and licked their lips in anticipation.

CHAPTER THIRTY-SEVEN

Santa Fe, New Mexico

The Santa Fe Public Library is housed in a 340-year-old building that once served as a monastery. The thick adobe walls, covered with ivory plaster and punctuated with colorful bursts of inlaid turquoise and other semi-precious stones, are festooned with historic drawings and photographs of the city.

Trixie knew at once where to begin her search. She drew down the thick treatise from the upper shelf and blew the dust off its upper binding. Obviously, Marcus Aaron's last published work, *Key to the Anasazi*, was not in great demand.

She looked up Tuzigoot in the index. *Bingo*. It was referenced four times, the first on page eighty-six. Quickly, she paged there. The relevant passage read:

> "Many fetishes glorify Tuzigoot, god of industry. These fetishes are remarkable in that, unlike all others, those of Tuzigoot do not resemble any animal or plant, but instead, picture the skyline of that ancient city."

Trixie searched for a clue in the remaining pages of the text, but came up with nothing.

She next found a detailed map of New Mexico. No Tuzigoot listed. After unsuccessfully searching several maps, she found a book on Indian ruins published by the University of New

Mexico. Tuzigoot was listed. She quickly paged to the section listing the ruin, and read:

> "Tuzigoot. This ruin, the remains of what is believed to be an ancient Anasazi regional center, was abandoned about 20 A.D. As with all other Anasazi sites, nothing is known as to where the inhabitants relocated or why they abandoned the city. The city was largely intact until 1599, when it was discovered by Vasquez de Gama, who leveled it, believing such action would be looked upon favorably by the Church. The most intact portion of the ruin is a series of foundations representing 59 interconnecting rectangular rooms. The foundations vary from one to four feet in height, and are perched high atop Blue Mesa near Socorro. Access is by dirt road off Rural Route 38; all terrain vehicles are strongly recommended."

Where was Socorro? Trixie re-consulted her New Mexico map, and had little trouble finding the town, which appeared to be west of Roswell, New Mexico, in the southern part of the state. Next, she obtained a detailed topographic map of the area surrounding Socorro. After a few minutes, she located the ruins, which were clearly marked atop Blue Mesa. It looked as if a single road led there.

She picked up Marcus's treatise. Reading Marcus's book was the next best thing to being with him. She opened the front cover and would have laughed if it had been funny. As she had surmised, almost no one had checked the book out the entire time it had been in circulation. In fact, the signature card reflected but one name: "K. Darstow, FBI."

CHAPTER THIRTY-EIGHT

Tuzigoot Ruin, New Mexico

It was tricky landing the shuttle among the rocky crags of the ruin, and there were a few moments when Professor Marcus Aaron was sure he was going to damage the craft. After a few tries, however, he managed to set the shuttle down at the far-east end of the ruin, near the abandoned well. There was at least ten feet of clearance on all sides, and the site was partially obscured by a grove of majestic cottonwood trees.

If Mariah had received his message, he was certain she would be followed. Therefore, it was imperative that he intercept her at the earliest opportunity, before Darstow and company could seize the shuttle. To that end, he would need to hide the shuttle somewhere with sufficient clearance for him to make a fast escape.

He had all night to find the best place.

While the Deminians apparently preferred to communicate telepathically among themselves, they had not learned to direct their machines that way. Consequently, the shuttle and the ship, as well as all the equipment contained in them, operated through touch control or voice direction.

Once he had accessed the ship's main computer bank, even he was amazed at the speed he had become fluent in Deminian. He had never learned a language so quickly, and soon he spoke and read it almost as if it was his native tongue. However, to prevent any misdirection that could arise from his still woefully incomplete understanding of Deminian history, technology, and culture, Marcus decided to generally direct all shuttle and ship operations in English. It had taken him over a year to reprogram the computers to recognize and act upon directions in the English language, a feat only made possible by his stumbling upon various technical manuals in the ship's enormous computer library.

The light from the shuttle's interior flashed across the mesa as he slid open the access hatch to exit the craft. The air was brisk, with a pungent scent of pine, and he nearly shivered with anticipation. Would Mariah arrive with the kids? He hoped she would be accompanied by Trixie.

Marcus fitted his night vision goggles to his eyes and closed the hatch by passing his hand across a photosensitive cell in the shuttle's exterior wall. The hatch could only be opened by coded voice command or by touching in sequence a series of cleverly hidden photo cells recessed near the hatch. It had taken his team of linguists and engineers years to discover the correct sequence to open the hatch, so he was relatively confident that any stranger coming upon the shuttle would be unable to access it before he returned.

No one appeared to be about, and he would have been surprised to see anyone. However, it was not beyond the realm of possibility that campers would be on hand, and to make sure he was alone, he had scanned the ruins for animal life before landing. No humans had been detected, although numerous animals had been identified, including several coyotes, over a dozen rattlesnakes, and a large owl.

The path leading up to the main ruin was well-marked, and he set out at a brisk pace. Mariah would enter the site at the west end, where the only road leading to the ruin abruptly ended. It was doubtful that Darstow would pursue by air; there was no place to land anything larger than a hang glider, and a helicopter could be heard miles before it arrived. That meant Darstow would have to attack by land. Marcus had no doubt Darstow would position snipers throughout the ruin in an effort to kill or wound him. Anything to get his hands on the shuttle.

But Marcus had something even Darstow was unprepared for; a weapon neither Darstow nor any living human being had ever seen. If pressed, he would use that weapon on the great Keenan Darstow, and anyone else that got in the way.

CHAPTER THIRTY-NINE

Tuzigoot Ruin, New Mexico

There had been a flash of light at the end of the small dirt road intersecting the one upon which his car was stranded. The smaller road seemed to lead up to the top of an imposing mesa. Perhaps there were some people on the mesa who could summon help. Andrew's hair still stood on end, and as he hiked up the road, each follicle seemed to stiffen as he trudged towards the mesa's crest.

What the bullocks was going on?

It took him a good twenty minutes to reach the crest. Sweating heavily and completely out of breath, he didn't realize what he had stumbled upon until he tripped over a low foundation and broke through a string of flagging surrounding an undisturbed corner of an ancient ruin.

My God. What a fantastic place.

A harvest moon lit up the vast expanse of the ruin. It was absolutely silent, and although he was not a superstitious man, he began to feel the same foreboding he always experienced in a cemetery.

Suddenly, the mesa lit up to his left. As he glanced that way, Andrew thought he could make out something metallic at the far east end of the ruin behind a stand of tall trees. He began jogging towards the light, but after a few moments it expired. He slowed his pace to account for the darkness and some decidedly rougher terrain.

Andrew crept up to the stand of trees behind which the light had shone. He peered intently into the brush, but could see nothing. Slowly, so as to make as little noise as possible, he continued through the trees, stopping intermittently to listen. He heard nothing, other than an occasional gust of wind.

And there it was, perhaps six meters tall and about half that wide. Glistening brilliantly in the moonlight, pitched on its side. A silvery rocket!

Andrew leaped back into the brush and fumbled for his camera at the same time. *Oh God, oh God. Please let the batteries work.* On his hands and knees, he crawled up to the clearing where the rocket lay, and waited for the flash unit to charge.

The batteries were dead. How was he going to prove what he was witnessing? No one would believe he had seen a rocket without pictures, and even if he had pictures, many would claim they were fraudulent.

The rocket was shaped like a thumb cut off square at the first knuckle. There were no windows or doors that he could see. There didn't appear to be any movement inside, but if the rocket was of substantial mass, any movement within certainly wouldn't shift it. The sudden realization that he may have stumbled upon an alien spacecraft nearly overcame his inclination to study the rocket further.

Ever so slowly, Andrew crawled up to the rear of the rocket. Its skin was smooth and cool to the touch, rather like aluminium. Carefully, he placed his left ear to the skin, but heard no sounds from inside.

Trying his best to make as little sound as possible, Andrew crawled around the entire perimeter of the ship, and scanned the skin, as best he could, for some break or line evidencing an entry-way or portal. He found nothing.

He performed the same routine again, this time standing erect. Still, he found no break in the rocket's skin. Indeed, the skin was as smooth as glass, with no detectable imperfections.

Perhaps the rocket was accessed from the roof. But how the blazes could he get up there? No rocks surrounding the rocket were of sufficient height to allow him to climb. But a thick branch of one of the adjoining trees nearly touched the top of the craft. All he had to do was climb the tree, scoot out onto the branch, and somehow swing or jump onto the rocket's roof. It would have been child's play, if he was a child. But forty-eight years of Guinness and kidney pie had taken its toll on his physique. His doubts about his abilities grew with each meter of the tree he scaled.

Bloody and tired almost beyond his experience, Andrew reached the branch overhanging the rocket. He perched there for nearly ten minutes, until his breathing normalized and most of his strength returned to his arms.

The concept of scooting out onto the branch seemed less plausible seven meters off the ground. He certainly couldn't walk out onto the branch, and he didn't have the strength to traverse the distance hand-over-hand. He had no choice. He would have to scoot.

Everything was fine until he lost his balance. Then, before he could counterbalance, he slipped to the left. He would have fallen free of the branch but for the fact he had unconsciously hooked his feet together. For a moment, he hung upside down. Then, summoning all his remaining strength, he swung his portly torso up high enough to grasp the branch with his interlocked hands. He then inched down the remaining distance like a sloth. What was remarkable was that in this position, the desired movement was incredibly easy.

But swinging out to the rocket was another matter. He was certain he could not reach the rocket by swinging from his locked feet. That meant he would have to release his leg hold, reverse direction, and then swing out to the craft, which was a good meter past the stubbed end of the branch. He knew he didn't have it in him to complete the maneuver. On the other hand, he wasn't sure he could even make it back up the branch, let alone reposition himself to climb down the trunk.

He didn't have to consider his dilemma for more than a few seconds. For there, immediately below him, stood an alien shaped much like a man but with huge, bulbous eyes that glowed bright green. The last thing Andrew remembered before he fainted were those horrible eyes, starring unblinking as he hurtled towards them.

CHAPTER FORTY

Medicine Stone Lake, New Mexico

Staring into the roaring fire, Dov could almost forget the circumstances that had led him here. Old Vic sat in an ancient rocker, chewing a thick wad of *Lieberman's Pure Leaf*, and spitting the dark juice into a tarnished spittoon at his feet. Jacob was curled up on an old sofa across the room next to the fireplace, leafing through some dog-eared *Field and Stream* issues published long before he was born.

Thomas lay flat on his back in front of the fire, his head resting against Boris's massive shoulder. Apparently, the bear had taken quite a liking to Thomas and followed him everywhere. This was in stark contrast to Waldo, who snarled at everyone except Old Vic, to whom he was totally devoted. Dov had steered clear of both bears, despite Vic's repeated assurances that he had nothing to fear since the bears only attacked strangers. Or so he said.

They had decided that Dov and Thomas would return to Santa Fe to rendezvous with Trixie Pentov. Jacob would stay at Medicine Stone. "Damn it, I don't want no kid here," Vic had protested. But Dov could tell, from the old man's eyes, that he really wanted the boy to stay. Earlier in the evening, Jacob had asked Vic about the tackle they were going to use during the following morning's fish, and Vic had become noticeably enthused. Jacob would be in good hands, despite the old man's penchant for swearing.

"I think its time to put the kid to sleep," Thomas volunteered.

"Boy can stay up as late as he wants," Vic spat. "When you was here, I never made you go to bed at partic'lar time."

"Yeah, and look at what a ruined life it led to," Thomas responded. "Let's go kid."

Jacob looked up at Thomas, and seeing he had no choice, got up and tramped down to the guest room adjacent to Old Vic's. Thomas followed him in to get him settled.

"So, yer FBI?" Vic asked Dov, barely raising an eyebrow.

"Assistant Director, Criminal Investigation Division."

"That a purty good job?"

"Yes. At least until this mess."

"I didn't think they'd let a Jew in there, much less an Israeli."

"I'm a naturalized U.S. citizen. My family left Israel when I was fourteen."

"Still, yer a Jew, and Hoover always thought Jews were Communists, at least that's what people said."

"The Bureau was full of anti-Semitic people when I first became an agent. But attitudes have dramatically changed over the past few years. People like me are now given an equal shot with the rest."

Old Vic said nothing further, choosing instead to just stare into the dancing flames of burning mesquite.

As Thomas re-entered, Old Vic asked, "Why do you want to hook up with this lady professor?"

Thomas drew himself up to the fire to warm his hands.

Dov said, "My job was to find Thomas and the boy and then return to discover what Dr. Pentov had learned about this Tuzigoot."

"Yeah, you said that, and it didn't register with me until now." Vic stared for a moment into Dov's eyes. "I know what Tuzigoot is."

Both Dov and Thomas gave the old man their full attention.

With difficulty, Vic pushed himself from the rocker and walked over to a large topographical map of New Mexico displayed above the mantel of the fireplace. "Come over here," he gestured.

Dov and Thomas crowded around expectantly.

Vic scanned the map for a moment and then pointed his gnarled index finger at the southwest corner. "There's your mysterious Tuzigoot," he snapped.

Though they stared at the place indicated, neither Dov nor Thomas saw anything resembling Tuzigoot.

"There's nothing that says Tuzigoot there," Thomas retorted. He looked at Dov for confirmation. Dov nodded his assent.

"I di'nt say it said 'Tuzigoot,'" Vic murmured in disgust. "I jes said that's where the damn place is."

"Well how do you know Tuzigoot's on that mesa?" Thomas asked.

"Long while ago, about when I was young Jacob's age, my Pa took me 'round New Mexico. We hiked and camped just about everywhere." Vic returned to his rocker, and drew an old clay pipe to his thin lips.

"I cin remember the place jest like it was yesterday. There was an old dirt road that led up the mesa. Boy it was a hike. And when the road ends, it opens up into a vast ruin. Vast, like Canyon de Chelly, except all the pueblo walls are mostly knocked down."

"So, Tuzigoot is an Indian ruin?" Thomas asked.

Vic nodded, drawing deep on his glowing pipe. "Anasazi, my Pa said. Looked awful old. The mesa is surrounded by high canyon walls, so while it rises above the landscape, it seems as if yer far below level ground." Vic laughed. "Kind of a mysterious place, I tell ya. We camped there just one night, but I 'member not sleeping very well; thought them Anasazi would come looking for me in the night."

Dov glanced at Thomas. "There couldn't be more than one place called Tuzigoot. That's got to be it."

Thomas nodded. "Well, we should try to hook up with your Professor Pentov anyway, just in case." He turned and left the room.

Dov sat down at the massive oak dinner table and wrote down the coordinates of the mesa, noting that the closest big town was Socorro. Perhaps they could retain a guide there, who could show them just where the mesa was located. "I'm hitting the sack," he announced.

Vic didn't respond, but he didn't think that was unusual. He didn't notice anything unusual until it was too late to react.

CHAPTER FORTY-ONE

Santa Fe, New Mexico

It started to drizzle as Trixie exited the new rental car she had leased from the Hilton. She drew up her collar, lifted her skirt to prevent the hem from being spotted, and dashed for the front door. No one answered the bell, and the door was locked.

Without quite knowing why, she slipped around the back of the adobe, trying to gain access through a door or window. All appeared latched in place or covered by immovable screens. Why had Mariah left? She said she'd stay home until Trixie could explain the meaning of Tuzigoot. The rain had ceased, for the moment, and Trixie sat down in one of Mariah's twisted willow patio chairs to sort out her thoughts. It was eerily quiet.

A few seconds, perhaps minutes passed. And then out of the mist she heard what sounded like faint, rapid breathing.

Quickly, she turned about, but saw nothing. The breathing was coming from the west end of the back yard, where Mariah's bedroom was located. Slowly, she made her way to the area where the noise originated. Guided more by the sound rather than her eyes, Trixie saw nothing until she was almost upon it. And when she saw it, she burst into tears.

Mariah's tiny dog Muffin was lying on its side, panting rapidly, and unable to move. A small trickle of blood dripped from its mouth. Gathering the dog in her arms, Trixie inspected it for wounds, but found none. The dog appeared to have sustained some internal injury, and it gasped in pain when she lifted it to her breast and hurried to the car.

In a panic, Trixie threw the car into reverse and headed to town, hoping to spy a veterinary clinic en-route. Muffin lay on the passenger seat and starred blankly ahead with glassy brown eyes.

A fine rain hit the windshield, making visibility more difficult in the deepening dusk. She saw nothing but houses, endless blocks of adobe, punctuated by an occasional antique store or small grocery. And with each passing mile, Muffin's breathing grew fainter.

"Michael Anthony, M.D., Internal Medicine," read the small sign in front of an unimposing territorial to her right. Not knowing what else to do, Trixie jammed on the brakes and skidded to a stop in front of Dr. Anthony's office. It was well after five o'clock, but there were lights on in the office.

The front door was of some dark, polished wood. Finding no doorbell, Trixie pounded on the door with all her strength. Hearing no response, she continued until her right hand began to bruise.

"All right, damn it." a man bellowed from behind the door.

"Please, Doctor, it's an emergency." Trixie shouted. The door opened to reveal a tall, muscular but balding man in jeans and a T-shirt that said, "Support your Right to Arm Bears."

"Dr. Anthony?"

"How can I help you?"

"I found an injured dog. I'm afraid it won't live if it doesn't receive treatment in a few minutes."

"Heck, I'm not a vet," the doctor snapped. "I'm not competent to examine him."

He tried to shut the door.

Trixie grasped the physician's hand. "Please, Doctor, this dog is owned by a dear friend. Can't you at least look at it?"

The doctor's face softened. "Where is he?"

Trixie brightened. "She. In the car. I'll go get her."

"Bring her into the examining room to the left off the reception area," Dr. Anthony said as he retreated into the office.

The examining room was crowded with the usual medical equipment, as well as dozens of articles tacked to the wall explaining why physicians made you wait hours for appointments and why national health care and HMOs were disastrous ideas. Muffin lay quietly on the examining table, breathing more rapidly than ever.

"Okay, let's see what's wrong with her," Dr. Anthony said, as he strode into the room and slipped on some thin latex gloves. He slowly moved his hands over the little dog's torso, looking into the animal's eyes to see if his probing fingers caused a reaction. "Doesn't seem to be any wounds," he murmured. Turning Muffin on her back, the doctor began probing her belly. The dog immediately convulsed in pain.

"Look's like she ate something that is blocking her intestinal passage. Let's take a quick pic." The doctor placed the little dog in a small plastic tray, which he positioned under a small X-ray machine attached to the far end of the wall.

"I usually use this for breast exams," he quipped.

Trixie smiled.

The doctor took two views of the dog's abdomen, the first with Muffin laying on her back and the second with the dog on her left side. After the film was exposed, the doctor left the room to develop it, and motioned for Trixie to have a seat.

"I can't sit," she apologized.

"Suit yourself," the doctor said. "I think I have an encyclopedia with a cutaway view of a dog's anatomy. That will have to do if we have to operate." With that, he turned and walked out of the room.

Muffin's eyes had begun to glaze over with a thin yellow film.

Trixie lovingly stroked the poor animal's coat, telling her she would be fine. The dog began to shiver, and its tongue became extended. "What's taking so long?" she called out.

"You understand. I will not be responsible for this dog." The physician's stern voice had momentarily startled her.

"Yes, of course."

Dr. Anthony starred into Trixie's eyes to accentuate his admonition. "Unless you have a strong stomach, you should leave the room." Trixie nodded and returned to the reception area, where she tried to read the doctor's six-month-old issues of *Guns and Ammo*.

It was more than an hour before Dr. Anthony returned to the reception area. His white lab coat was splattered with flecks of blood, but he was smiling.

"How is she?"

"She's alive. I don't know if she'll make it, but she appears stable. I gave her a little dose of morphine to relax her."

"Did you find what had blocked her intestine?"

"I wanted to talk to you about that," said the doctor. He exited the room and returned with a plastic box about the size of a paperback book.

"The dog had swallowed what looks like some sort of tiny key. It's of an incredibly strange design, like none I've ever seen. Part of the key had lodged itself in the stomach wall, where it had caused a small hemorrhage. I managed to suture up the cut tissues without much trouble." Dr. Anthony grinned. "Did one hell of a job for a beginner, I'd say."

The doctor's enthusiasm was fetching, and Trixie smiled as well. "Can I see the key?"

"That's the rub, you see," said the doctor. I can't show it to you, at least not directly."

Caught off guard, Trixie stammered. "Well, uh…why… why can't I see it?"

Dr. Anthony fixed his eyes on Trixie. "After I withdrew the key from the dog, I wiped it dry and set it in a specimen dish. I turned my attention to the dog. As I was suturing her up, an intense, white light flashed from the specimen dish, as if the key in it had been consumed by fire. And then the most bizarre thing happened." Dr. Anthony looked down at his hands.

Trixie waited. After a few uncomfortable moments, she gently touched the doctor's arm and said, "What was bizarre?"

Startled, Dr. Anthony opened up the plastic box and drew out a glass specimen dish. "The key had been consumed by fire, you see, some sort of spontaneous combustion occurred. But the flash had traced an exact replica of the key's face into the bottom of this glass dish." He held the bottom of the dish up to the light so Trixie could see the imprint.

The trace was definitely that of a key, although it was highly angular, with many sharp cuts and grooves spiraling around both its shaft and head. The pattern made by the cuts and grooves did not appear to be in any recognizable style, but what looked like some sort of mathematical code ran the length of the shaft:

13.14.18.21.9.14/10X9X10X8-2

Bewildered, Trixie asked, "What do you think the numbers mean?"

"Your guess is as good as mine," Anthony responded. "But I'll tell you something else that was strange." He looked to see that he had Trixie's full attention.

"After I put the key into the specimen dish, I glanced at it. But I only saw the side of the key that was facing up. Of course, that side was not traced into the specimen dish when it burned away. But there were words on that side."

"Well, what were they?"

The doctor drew a pencil from his ear and carefully printed the following on a magazine cover separating them:

"On Top Of Their Dead."

CHAPTER FORTY-TWO

Medicine Stone Lake, New Mexico

"I don't think I've 'ad the pleasure, Agent Bar-Lev." It was an Irish voice, but frighteningly sinister in tone.

Dov looked up into the barrel of a Walther P8. The semiautomatic was gripped by none other than Piter Mentol, the notorious IRA terrorist. "Yer wondering how we found you?" Mentol sneered. "It was a simple matter. We tagged your motorcar with a beeper at the hotel where you dined with the lovely Dr. Pentov."

Summoning up his courage, Dov asked, "What do you intend to do with us?"

Mentol laughed, his voice almost shrieking with delight. "You, I will hold. I should be able to fetch quite a good price for you in Aqaba or Cali." He grinned widely, placing the pistol's barrel directly on Dov's forehead. "I don't care to see the boy or old man suffer, mind you. We shall kill them quick, painless."

Mentol's voice lowered an octave, growing more ominous. "But that Kuzmic, he and I have a score to settle, and I'm a mind to settle it on my terms and at his expense."

He took a step back and gestured for Dov to rise. As Dov obeyed, he glanced to his right, and saw that Old Vic was still asleep in his chair across from the blazing fire.

Mentol directed Dov to approach the fireplace directly across from Old Vic. As he reached the mantel, another man entered the room with Jacob by the arm. The boy was obviously still delirious with sleep, and didn't quite know what to make of the circumstances.

"I can't find Kuzmic," the henchman said, in an east-end clip.

Mentol reached into his overcoat and retrieved a portable radio transceiver. "Mentol to crew. Any sign of Kuzmic?"

Nothing but static could be heard until the radio blurted, "Nothing, yet. We'll find 'em."

"Remember, take 'im alive, if ya can," Mentol called into the handset. He thrust the device back into his pocket and motioned for his companion to place Jacob next to Dov. "We'll all wait here until the entire family is collected," he said. He looked down with disgust at Old Vic, who was still sleeping, oblivious to all that had transpired.

Suddenly, shots rang out, seeming to come from the side of the lodge. "Get out there," Mentol directed his henchman, with clenched teeth. The man obeyed, leaving them alone with Mentol, who had stepped back so as to better cover them. His back was to the kitchen.

"Ahhhhhhh!" The piercing scream had come from just behind Mentol, and as he turned toward the sound, Dov dove for Mentol's knees. Startled, Mentol tried to sidestep Dov's assault while bringing his pistol to bear upon the FBI agent's head, but Dov managed to catch Mentol's left ankle and pull the assassin to the floor. Two rounds exploded out of Mentol's gun, but both veered wide of their mark, the first ricocheting off the mantel and the second nearly hitting Old Vic's rocker.

"What the hell's damnation is going on here?" The old man bellowed, jolted awake by the gunplay.

Dov and Mentol struggled on the floor, with Dov trying to wrest control of Mentol's pistol and Mentol trying to shoot

Dov with it. Neither man was able to pummel the other with many blows, since their concentration was almost entirely directed at gaining control of Mentol's gun, which was waving wildly in his right hand.

With speed that defied his years, Vic sprang from the rocker and ran for the back porch with Jacob, who was in shock. "Run for the boathouse and take a boat out onto the lake," he directed, as he pushed the boy out the screen door. With that, he ran back into the lodge, narrowly dodging another round loosed from Mentol's gun.

As Dov and Mentol struggled, sometimes standing but more often on the floor, Vic tore into his bedroom and retrieved his old Winchester Model 1912. The shotgun was always fully loaded with four twelve-gauge shells, and he had little time to do anything but thumb off the safety before hearing another scream from the kitchen.

Vic entered the kitchen and saw Boris gorging on the remains of what must have been one of the assault team members. Another man, standing in the frame of the front door, which abutted the kitchen, had a horrified look on his face but tried to draw a bead on the bear's head. Vic shot the man without hesitation, blowing his torso out the door. The shot caused Boris to bolt upright. Vic knew enough not to get between the bear and his meal, and so he returned to the great room, just in time to see Mentol and Dov crash over a sofa and onto a knotted pine coffee table.

Try as he might, Vic couldn't get a good shot at Mentol, for he and Dov were hopelessly intertwined. A few times, Vic tried to hit Mentol on the head with the butt of the shotgun, but after accidentally swatting Dov, he abandoned such efforts.

The struggling men writhed over the carpet to the hearth, with Dov tightly gripping Mentol's pistol with one hand while trying to stave off Mentol's blows with the other. Both men were bruised, scratched, and bleeding. Finally, Mentol's gun was thrown loose, and Vic quickly retrieved it and thrust it into his waistband.

Mentol then bit Dov viciously on the cheek. Crying out, Dov raked Mentol's face with a powerful blow from his elbow, throwing Mentol to the floor on his back. Vic rushed over and shoved the barrel of the shotgun directly onto his nose. "Give it up Bozo," he said in a steely voice. His eyes wide with disgust, Mentol just blinked his submission.

"Throw me the handgun," Dov called out. Vic tossed the pistol, careful to keep the barrel of the shotgun pointed squarely at Mentol's chest.

"Don't worry about me," Vic offered. "Just find Tommy and bail his ass out if he needs a hand." With that, Vic ordered Mentol to the floor in front of the mantel. "I'm glad you showed up, boy," the old man said to Mentol. "I got years of stories to tell, and it looks like you are going to get to hear every one of 'em, maybe three or four times apiece."

Dov ran out the rear door of the lodge, keeping close to the lodge wall for cover. Turning west, he jogged up the path towards the guest cabins that ran perpendicular to the lake. As he ran, he ejected and checked the magazine from Mentol's pistol, noting there were only six rounds left.

He checked each of the cabins, but found no sign of Thomas, much less any of Mentol's henchmen. Perhaps someone could be found around the barn at the front of the lodge.

Reversing course, Dov hurried toward the barn, running as low to the ground as he could. Before he reached the front clearing, two of Mentol's men exited the barn. Both men carried laser sighted Steyr-Aug automatic rifles, which were incredibly accurate at a range of less than 100 yards. Dov sprang into the brush lining the side of the path. His Walther pistol was no match for the firepower of his opponents, and he doubted he could drop more than one of the men before being cut to ribbons by the other.

The men began walking directly towards Dov, as if they saw him. A fear like no other gripped him. *This was it,* he thought. *I'm about to be killed.*

An overwhelming peace rolled over Dov. Without thinking, he leaped out of the brush towards the men, his pistol blazing. "By God, I'll not die hiding!" he screamed, loosing all six rounds in no more than two seconds.

One round hit the man at the right in the upper thigh and sent him sprawling. His rifle flew over his right shoulder. All the other shots sprayed wide, and as Dov's gun locked open upon expelling the last round, the remaining man raised his rifle to sever Dov in half. Dov shut his eyes as the bullets rang out.

Funny, he thought. *I can hear the bullets hit me, and they don't even hurt. I must be dead.* He opened his eyes. His executioner lay in a pool of blood at his feet.

"You're definitely a desk jockey," Thomas told Dov as he threw Dov the dead man's rifle.

Thomas approached the man Dov had wounded, who writhed on the ground in pain. As Thomas drew nearer, the man managed to pull a menacing knife from his boot and attempted to slash Thomas several times. Without fanfare, Thomas placed a single round from his Uzi directly into the man's forehead that killed him instantly.

"Hell, I didn't want to carry him into the lodge anyway," he said. "Let's get back there and see if Old Vic needs our help."

As they walked away, Waldo emerged from behind a juniper bush and began nosing the bloody corpses.

"You know," Thomas laughed, smirking. "I think it's going to take Old Vic quite awhile to get them back to a diet of just fish and berries."

Kuzmic's macabre humor was lost on Dov. All he could think of was Trixie Pentov. *Had she been spared?*

CHAPTER FORTY-THREE

Tuzigoot Ruin, New Mexico

When Andrew first awoke, he didn't know where he was. Then it all came back: the rocket, the alien, the fall. He nearly passed out again as the shocking memories flooded his brain.

His heart pumping, Andrew frantically searched for the alien. Its body lay crumpled in a heap not a meter from where Andrew sat. With considerable effort, he drew himself up, and mustering all his courage, gingerly approached the alien. It appeared to have human form, except for a strange apparatus encircling its head. And then it moved.

Andrew retreated back, searching for cover. The alien made faint moaning sounds, and before Andrew had time to react, reared up on its knees. Andrew gasped. That caused the alien to direct its full attention on the journalist, who was gripped by a bizarre combination of fascination and fear. Helpless, half-expecting to be killed, Andrew starred unblinking as the alien slowly removed the apparatus on its head.

"Who are you?" it asked. The voice was that of an ordinary man, an American at that.

Andrew was unable to respond.

The alien stepped toward Andrew, who recoiled, tripping over a log and falling on his back. Before Andrew could stand, the alien bent over him. It looked perfectly human; just like a sixty-year old man, bald, with a trim salt-and-pepper beard, and intense blue eyes.

The alien extended his hand to Andrew, who took it in spite of his fear. The alien drew Andrew up and dusted him off.

"Well now, since you've nearly crushed me, how about telling me your name?" it said gently.

"S...S...Sawyer, Andrew Sawyer, of the...the *Times*," Andrew sputtered.

The alien studied him. "A reporter?"

"Ye...yes. We prefer to be called journalists."

The alien dropped its head a moment, as if to think. "Well, I guess we're going to be married for awhile," it murmured. "My name is Aaron, Marcus Aaron."

Seeing that meant nothing to the journalist, Aaron explained, "I'm a professor of linguistics, formerly of the University of Chicago."

Andrew brightened. "So you're not from a different planet?"

"What made you think that?" the Professor asked.

"Well, the rocket, of course. And that headset you were wearing when I first spotted you."

"Oh, the night vision gear. It's quite useful in places such as this." Aaron raised his long arms, waving his hands at the far walls of the canyon.

"What are you doing here?" Andrew's natural curiosity stifled any remaining apprehension about his newfound companion.

The Professor drew away, turned his back on the journalist, and said nothing for several seconds, as if weighing his options. "Empty your pockets," he ordered.

Surprised, Andrew did nothing.

"Empty your pockets, and prove to me you are who you say."

Grudgingly, Andrew complied by tossing his billfold, the rental car keys, and his Eton pen at the Professor's feet.

Aaron gathered up the effects and moved to an area directly exposed to a shaft of moonlight. He studied the contents of Andrew's billfold intently.

"What is the *Tattler?*" he queried.

"Oh, that's just a tabloid I occasionally write for."

"How come you have no corresponding identification for the *Times?*"

"It isn't in there?" Andrew said, feigning surprise. "Oh *now* I remember, I accidentally left it at the air base in Magdalena, when the guard requested it." He tried to discern from the Professor's face whether his lies were working, but Aaron's eyes were masked by the dark.

"Why did you visit the base at Magdalena?"

Andrew decided to take a chance. "I believe the Americans have developed a new space-based laser weapon. The weapon blinds all that cross its path. The Americans have tested it successfully in many locations throughout Asia."

"How do you know the Americans have developed this weapon?" the Professor asked.

"No other nation has the means of deploying it. Russia is in shambles, and no European or Asian power has either the money or the technology to do it."

"Assuming the Americans have developed and deployed such a system, how does that lead you to this lonely canyon in southern New Mexico?"

Andrew chuckled. He stepped toward the Professor, and wrapped his meaty arms around the man's broad shoulders. "Actually, it all started with a matchbook in my flat."

* * *

Mariah had been hooded for what seemed an eternity. Occasionally, she heard faint noises, as the van in which she had been placed crossed over railroad tracks, cattle guards or bad roads. But most of the time, she sat in silence, with her handcuffed wrists folded on her lap. The men, or perhaps women, accompanying her rarely spoke, even when she asked them where they were going or if they could make a bathroom stop. This last request was honored in a fashion. They pulled her from the vehicle and told her to urinate behind some foliage.

If only she hadn't lost the key. She had kept it on a thin gold chain encircling her neck ever since it had arrived in the sweepstakes envelope forwarded by the Professor. Her instinct had been to keep the key secret, even from Darstow. And now that her betrayal by Darstow had become clear, when her need for the key may have been most important, she had lost it. It must have been torn loose during the struggle, when she had been overpowered in her bed by Russo and Leland.

The van veered to the left and then slowed. Eventually, it stopped, and the ignition was killed. The side door slid open, and they yanked her out. She tripped as she missed the van's running board and fell to the ground, which felt like gravel.

"Unhood her." The voice was that of Keenan Darstow.

Rough hands reached up her back and slipped the knots securing the rope holding the hood in place. As the hood was ripped off, she was temporarily blinded by the sunlight, which seemed to be gathering into dusk.

"Welcome to *Brunton Lodge*," Darstow said sarcastically.

They were standing in the drive fronting a stone house that seemed quite old-- perhaps dating back to the 1880s.

Darstow led Mariah and her escorts, Agents Leland and Russo, into the lodge, which was furnished in Victorian antiques. Numerous oil paintings lined the walls, and heavy red velvet drapes shrouded the windows.

"Why have you kidnapped me?" Mariah demanded.

Darstow laughed. "You and Pentov thought you were so clever. Hiding in the bathroom, telling each other your little secrets, planning your little plans. We heard everything."

"You bugged my bathroom?" Mariah stared incredulous. "Did you have a warrant to do that?"

Leland let out a chuckle, which Darstow silenced by darting him a menacing look.

"To paraphrase the banditos from my favorite movie, my dear, I don't need no stinking warrant, even to wire your toilet. But enough of the twenty questions. I assume you want to see your daughter?"

Mariah's mood brightened. "Oh yes," she pleaded.

Russo unlocked her handcuffs and led her into a small bedroom. She sensed her daughter before seeing her. The girl lay curled up in a ball at the end of a bed tucked against a white plaster wall. The room's windows were barred.

"You have till morning," Russo intoned.

"What then?"

Russo looked down at the floor, as to avoid Mariah's gaze. "Then your ordeal ends."

CHAPTER FORTY-FOUR

Tuzigoot Ruin, New Mexico

They had decided to take Mentol's Rover since it had four-wheel capability and was equipped with a two-way radio they hoped was tuned to Darstow's communications frequency. Thomas had taken the first shift at the wheel. Dov had quickly fallen asleep as they tore through the night on the lonely interstate.

Thomas caught himself smirking, replaying Mentol's interrogation in his mind. He had seen scores of interrogations, some more "civilized" than others, but none as effective as that practiced by Old Vic.

They had strapped Mentol into one of the battered oak chairs strewn about the great room. When Mentol refused to answer their questions, Thomas had variously threatened to shoot him in the knees or cut off his fingers. Mentol had just cursed them with an unending string of expletives, confident that Thomas's threats were empty. Finally, Old Vic had heard enough.

"You're not get'in anywhere with this one," he spat in disgust. "Leave 'em to me."

Mentol laughed aloud. "Non a you have the nerve to kill a helpless man in cold blood. Why waste your time, I'll tell ya nothing."

"Yer right," Vic said. "None of us, even Thomas, would fall to yer level, kill'n the helpless. But my bears...my bears will kill you without a second's thought, especially now they've tasted human blood."

"You can't let the bears have him." Dov pleaded. "We need to bring him back to Washington for interrogation and prosecution."

Vic shot Dov a disdainful glance. "This one is working for yer precious Bureau. My God, what makes you think anythin' will 'appen to 'im if you manage to even bring 'im back?"

"He's right, Dov," Thomas said. "The game's fixed, and Mentol is Darstow's knight; the whole Bureau is pitted against us."

Dov threw up his hands in resignation. "I suppose you're right."

Vic looked at Dov and Thomas. "You both better leave. It'll get messy."

Mentol's eyes grew larger as Thomas and Dov left the great room. Vic followed them out to the kitchen, returning with a jar of honey and a large serrated fillet knife. Without a word, he slit Mentol's right pant leg, baring his sickly white thigh. He then poured the honey all over Mentol's leg, deftly avoiding Mentol's efforts to kick him.

"When I git from here, old pig, I'll carve you into small pieces." he hissed.

Vic chuckled quietly. "You don' get it, do ye?" he said. "I'm going to watch my bears tear off yer legs and rip out yer groin."

The old man left again, and as soon as he exited the room, Mentol looked frantically about, hoping to find some way to free himself. His hands were firmly bound, and while he could move his legs a few centimeters, it might be hours before he could manage to loosen them sufficiently to attempt an escape.

A horribly fetid, musky odor filled the room. At first, he heard nothing. Then the huge beast was facing him, blasting its foul breath in his face through its gaping nostrils.

"Go away. Go away," he shrieked. But rather than becoming frightened, his screams seemed to heighten the bear's interest, and soon it began nosing his honey encrusted thigh.

The bear's long, black tongue lashed out, raking Mentol's bare leg. Shivering, Mentol began screaming uncontrollably, frightened to his core. The bear pushed Mentol over backwards, its gigantic hindquarters positioned over Mentol's abdomen, pinning his bare leg with its rapier length claws. It continued licking the terrified man's leg, but when Mentol attempted to kick at it with his other leg; it began biting into his bare thigh. Excited by the taste of Mentol's blood, the great carnivore began ripping out Mentol's flesh. Fighting waves of nausea, Mentol cried out in terror, "I'll tell all, all," he begged. "Get it off a me. Off a me!"

The three of them had been watching from the kitchen entry way, and Old Vic quickly drew the bear off with a large broom and a raw porterhouse steak. Mentol lay in a pool of blood, crimson bursts shooting from his upper thigh where the bear had nearly severed his femoral artery. He was a completely broken man, shrieking uncontrollably. After they had bound his wounds, and given him nearly a half bottle of whisky to dull the pain, he had answered their questions without hesitation.

There was no use returning to Santa Fe to retrieve Mariah or Trixie Pentov. Mentol had revealed that Darstow knew about Tuzigoot, and planned to bring Mariah there the following morning in an effort to capture Mariah's father. While they had found Mentol's tale incredible, it fit the facts as they knew them. Apparently, Dr. Aaron had stolen an alien spacecraft with incredible destructive power, and Mariah's children had been kidnapped simply as a ruse to draw Aaron out of hiding so the spacecraft could be retrieved.

Thomas's smirk dimmed. "Darstow's certain to have an entire SWAT team on site to capture Aaron, and he would hold Mariah close to his position."

"Improvise."

"What?"

"We'll just have to improvise a solution," Dov explained.

"How did you know I was worried about that?" Thomas whispered.

"I'm worried too."

CHAPTER FORTY-FIVE

Santa Fe, New Mexico

"Why do we have to take all this stuff?" Trixie queried.

"Weren't you a Girl Scout?" Anthony asked. "We need this gear to be prepared for any eventuality."

"Well I'm not carrying most of this stuff," Trixie insisted. "Especially the guns and knives and all this other macho junk."

Anthony laughed. "You may rue the day, my dear Professor, that you shirked carrying a pistol."

Trixie rolled her eyes.

They had tossed what seemed like an entire arsenal into the bed of Anthony's battered station wagon. Having heard nothing from Dov, and having waited for him at the hotel well beyond the appointed hour, she decided to set off for Tuzigoot alone. As she was about to check out of the hotel, Anthony telephoned concerning Muffin's condition, offering to return the dog so it could recuperate at home. During the course of that conversation, and to her surprise, she had blurted out the entire story regarding the kidnapping of Mariah's children, the necklace, and Marcus Aaron's mysterious messages. Anthony had been intrigued, and despite her efforts to dissuade him, had insisted upon accompanying her to Tuzigoot.

They estimated the trip to the Tuzigoot mesa would take half the night. The plan was to drive as far as they could up the mesa's slope, and then walk the rest of the way to the summit, hoping to camp at the ruins before dawn.

As Anthony drove, Trixie retrieved the slip of paper upon which she had written the cryptic message burned into the petri dish:

13.14.18.21.9.14/10x9x10x8-2

"Obviously, this is some sort of code, probably written by Marcus and intended for Mariah," Trixie wondered aloud.

"Does Mariah speak any language other than English?" Anthony asked.

"No, so it's a fair bet the message represented by the code is in English. Mariah had no formal training in cryptology, so it also makes sense the code would be simple to solve."

Anthony thought a moment and said, "I agree. The simplest code would be to assign each letter of the alphabet a corresponding number. Thus, the letter A would be represented by the number 1, the letter B the number 2, and so on. Using this system, the first six letters of the code read: MNRUIN. Since we're bound for the Tuzigoot ruins, it seems logical to assume we should look for a main ruin."

Trixie interrupted. "But applying your system, the rest of the code is problematic, since the result spells: JIJH-B."

"Yeah, I don't know what that means," Anthony admitted.

"Wait, I've got an idea," Anthony offered. "What if the second half of the code is not meant to be representative of letters but instead, is intended to set forth various dimensions?"

"What do you mean?" Trixie asked.

"Suppose the second set of numbers is representative of dimensions, such as ten feet by nine feet by…Here, give me the paper." Anthony reached across Trixie's lap, grabbed the code, and held it above the steering wheel.

"Ten feet by nine feet by ten feet by eight feet" he exulted. "That's got to be it."

"Why do you think so?"

"X is often representative of the word 'by,' so it makes sense that's the meaning of that letter in the code."

"Assuming you're right that the second half of the code represents dimensions, how do you know those dimensions are in feet?"

Anthony frowned. "I don't. I imagine it could be meters, or even centimeters or yards or any other unit of linear measurement."

"If you're right," Trixie said, "the '-2' at the end of the code could mean 'two units of measure under' or it could mean the last unit of measurement given– '8,' is to be reduced by two units of measure."

Anthony laughed. "I've got a feeling we'll be unable to solve the riddle until we're at the ruin. Once there, the appropriate dimensions should become apparent to us."

"Your words to God's ear," Trixie muttered, thinking about Mariah, and then whimsically, Marcus.

Some time passed before either spoke.

"Don't forget the final message," Anthony said.

"What was that?"

"On Top Of Their Dead."

"I hope that reference is to the Anasazi."

CHAPTER FORTY-SIX

Tuzigoot Ruin, New Mexico

"You're insane." Andrew ranted.

Marcus paused. "I imagine there is some truth to that. But my options are limited. What would you have me do?"

Andrew just shook his head. "It's all so fantastic. Even the *Tattler* couldn't come up with something this bizarre."

"Timing will be important. You will be a great help, if you do precisely as I instructed."

Andrew sweated profusely. "But what if things go awry, and they find out I'm your accomplice. I'm not even an American citizen, by God. They will imprison me forever."

Marcus waited a few moments for the reporter to calm down. "If things go bad, Mr. Sawyer, prison is the least of your worries. Keenan Darstow has had scores of people killed, some with damn little reason. This time he has plenty of reasons to kill you, me, and every other innocent on hand. You must not doubt that for an instant."

"You're hardly an innocent Professor. You've killed hundreds of soldiers and airmen throughout Asia, all because you decided to play God and decide they should die so that others might live. How can you justify that? Oh, I know, the little green men made you do it."

"They aren't green."

The Professor turned toward an instrument panel, trying to avert Andrew's righteous stare.

"The Deminians didn't program me to kill those soldiers. Killing isn't condoned in their culture."

"Then why, Professor? Why have you, a man of culture, a man who has spent so many years investigating the best of humanity, become so inhuman?"

"I saw inequities, and wanted to balance the playing field. And in the process, it's true, I became what I loathed." The Professor turned to the journalist. "But now, my daughter and grandchildren are in danger, and I need your help to keep them safe."

"A danger of your own making."

"Yes, yes, of course. But there will be no more attacks and interventions. This place, this is my last stand. Today, I'm leaving this planet forever."

"Why today?"

"I'm dying Mr. Sawyer. Cancer. Terminal, in fact. And after rescuing my family from Keenan Darstow's clutches, they will either accompany me to Deminia in this ship, or I will fly there alone to spend my last days. And without access to this ship, Darstow, and the men for whom he acts, will no longer need to use my family as a lure to catch me. One thing is certain: I will not permit this ship to fall into Darstow's hands. He would compound my bad acts by a factor of ten. So, I beg you. Help me save my family, and in turn, this fair planet."

Andrew recalled his encounter with the gents who had attacked him and, no doubt, were Darstow's henchmen. At that moment, he committed himself to the Professor's cause, not so much because he cared for the man, but because he knew that if Darstow succeeded in capturing the shuttle, he would not let anyone know of its existence. And reporting the Professor's incredible tale was the break for which he'd been praying.

"After you're gone, I must have irrefutable proof of everything," Andrew insisted. "For my story."

Aaron pursed his lips. "Every evening, for these many years, I have dictated a log of my experiences both in the shuttle as well as on the larger ship. Will copies of these logs suffice?"

"They would be helpful, sure; but what proof are they, really? Don't you have something I could present to the scientific community to demonstrate that the logs are not fanciful?"

Aaron thought a moment and then reached into his pocket and produced three colored stones: one gold, one dark green, and the last a speckled white. He put them into Andrew's hand.

"What are these?"

"After I'm gone, and ONLY after I'm gone, assemble several eminent zoologists and place each of these under a warm lamp, or even in your mouth, for a few minutes. From them will spring life forms unknown to this planet that could not have evolved here."

Andrew was beside himself with delight. "But what are they? Will they harm anyone?"

Aaron smiled. "They are harmless, and will not live long, as you understand the concept. The Deminians call them 'Brighters,' and their sole purpose is to impart strength and happiness to those near them."

"How do they do that?"

"It's hard to explain," Aaron responded. "After hatching, the Brighters look like multi-colored caterpillars. They throw off a sort of psychic energy, which greatly improves the health and emotional state of persons nearby. I think the Deminians used them as a sort of psychic drug, and there are some indications that they became a bit addicted to them. In any event, the Brighters will only remain active for a few hours, but that will certainly be long enough for you to prove that your encounter with me was not fantasy."

"Well Professor, I think I've got the makings of a story of a lifetime, and we've got a deal. Now, if only I can live long enough to see it in print."

Aaron didn't respond, for his gaze was fixed on the western edge of the mesa. There, spiraling up with the gathering light of dawn was a dirty, brown cloud of dust. "They're here."

CHAPTER FORTY-SEVEN

Tuzigoot Ruin, New Mexico

They had slowly crept up the mesa during the early hours of the morning, outfitted in desert camouflage and light sniper gear. Hess's orders had been brief, albeit fantastic. "Seize the alien craft, at all cost."

He had not been told anything about the craft, except that it was piloted by a renegade professor who had stolen it from an air force research installation years ago. If possible, his team was to capture the professor alive, but it had been made clear that was only a secondary concern. For the first time in his career, Colonel Samuel Hess was frightened. Not by the mission, or even what it concerned. No, it was the AD's admonition at the conclusion of the briefing:

"One more thing, Colonel."

"Yes sir." Hess stood at attention, as the AD glowered at him from an ornate desk in the little cottage where they had originally bivouacked.

"This mission is of utmost importance."

Hess did not respond.

"Failure will not be…tolerated."

It was the way he had said the last word. As if failure would spell his death.

* * *

"No. Don't touch her."

Mariah lashed out at Russo, who had stolen into their darkened room and pulled the golden-haired Brittany from the bed they shared.

Russo slapped Mariah away with the back of his hand, bloodying her nose. Nevertheless, she came at the agent again, clawing at him with her nails. Her tenacity caught Russo off guard, and as he attempted to ward her off, Brittany ran out the room.

Russo then flung himself at Mariah, blocked her flailing arms, and tackled her to the floor. He then flipped her on her stomach and handcuffed her hands behind her back.

Mariah hoped Brittany had escaped.

"Fighting us is useless, and as you've discovered, painful." The voice was of Keenan Darstow himself.

Mariah turned her head toward Darstow's voice. Behind her, framed in the doorway, Darstow and Leland held onto Brittany, who was also handcuffed.

Russo pulled Mariah to her feet.

"Fit her," Darstow commanded.

Leland left the room and returned with a matchbook size black box attached to a thick red strap. He wound the strap around Brittany's thin neck, with the buckle clasped at the back and the box positioned at her throat.

"What's that?" Mariah asked, clearly distressed.

"That," Darstow said, "is my 'Maker.'"

Mariah gave Darstow a perplexed look.

"A Maker?"

Leland chuckled, but quickly stopped after Darstow gave him a disapproving glance.

"This little box is going to *make* you do exactly what I tell you," Darstow said, as he gestured to the black box under Brittany's chin.

"And…how is that?" Mariah whispered.

Darstow retrieved a larger black box from his coat pocket. It had a black, graphite antennae at the top, and a red button on its face. Darstow stroked Brittany's fine blonde hair. The girl shivered.

"The box at your precious daughter's throat is a small, but potent explosive device. It is going to make you do what I say, exactly as I say." Darstow's voice lowered, "Because if you do not follow my instructions to the letter, I will depress a button, and the device at your daughter's neck will punch a hole the size of a baseball through her throat."

CHAPTER FORTY-EIGHT

Tuzigoot Ruin, New Mexico

"Don't blame me," Thomas snapped.

"*You* wanted to take the bastard's Rover," Dov responded. "If we had taken the rental, it would have had a spare."

"Who would have thought a $50,000 SUV wouldn't have a spare?" Thomas responded.

Dov shook his head. They had suffered the flat not fifteen miles from the dirt road that lead to the mesa. They had searched the Rover from top to bottom, but no spare tire could be found.

"We'll just have to flag someone down," Thomas said.

Dov gestured toward the empty highway. "And who might that be? We haven't seen a soul since we've been on this godforsaken stretch."

Thomas groaned.

"We'll just have to hoof it."

Resignedly, Thomas nodded, throwing open the rear door of the Rover and collecting the essential arms and supplies.

"If we've read the necklace right, we've just got a few hours."

Thomas threw Dov an H&K Sp10, slinging his favorite Uzi over his shoulder. "Then there's no time to waste."

CHAPTER FORTY-NINE

Tuzigoot Ruin, New Mexico

"A Tell," Trixie murmured.

"A what?"

"A Tell. The message, 'On Top Of Their Dead' may be a reference to a Tell."

"What the hell is a Tell?" Anthony asked, clearly irritated.

"They're mounds found throughout the Middle East. They're created by one generation of people literally building on top of the homes and businesses of their predecessors, so that if you excavate the sites, you can uncover relics from several different eras, maybe even different civilizations, the deeper you dig."

"Well, what do the Tells have to do with the message?"

"Many Tells are built upon graves. Early peoples often kept their dead near them, rather than far away, as is the modern custom. The reference to 'On Top Of Their Dead' may be a reference to the area of the Tell in which bodies are buried."

Anthony looked skeptical. "This isn't Israel or Egypt, Professor. And if I remember my Indian lore from the Boy Scouts, the Southwestern tribes like the Navajo disposed of their dead away from their villages. And most did not bury their dead, but placed them in hard-to-reach crevices in distant canyons."

Trixie digested Anthony's comments. "That may be true," she said. "But according to Marcus's book, Tuzigoot is not a

Navajo or Hopi ruin-- it's Anasazi, a tribe far more ancient, and about whom very little is known."

"Okay. Assuming you're right, and the Anasazi buried their dead at the ruin, how are we going to locate those graves?"

Trixie shook her head. "I don't have that worked out yet."

"Jesus. Look at those guys." Anthony pointed to two heavily-armed men jogging down the road in front of them.

Trixie grasped Anthony's arm so tightly he nearly veered off the road. "Stop." she yelled. "Stop the car."

Against his better judgment, Anthony slammed on the brakes and skidded to a stop in front of the men who, to his consternation, had leveled what looked like automatic weapons at the car's windshield. Before Anthony could react, Trixie leaped from the car, waving joyously.

"Dov, it's me, Trixie."

Dov smiled, lowered his gun, and embraced her. Anthony remained in the car, unsure who the mercenaries were.

"A pleasure to meet you, Dr. Pentov," Thomas bowed toward Trixie.

"I take it that was your Land Rover we saw a few miles back?" Anthony asked as he exited the car.

Thomas threw out his hand. "Thomas Kuzmic, private investigator." After they shook hands, Trixie introduced Dov to Anthony.

"And what do you do?" Dov asked Anthony.

"I'm a doctor."

"He knows everything," Trixie gushed. "Since Dov abandoned me, I needed someone to protect my *touchas*, and so the good doctor agreed to come along and solve the mystery."

Thomas gave Anthony the once over. "Ever had any military experience, particularly combat?"

"I served in Vietnam in the late 60s as a corpsman. Didn't see a lot of up-front, in-your-face action, but I stitched up my share of wounded and saw plenty of dead."

"And he's an incredible gun nut," Trixie interjected. "He has all sorts of weapons and appears to know how to use them."

"We might need a physician, if all goes to hell in a handbasket," Dov said.

"Can you fit us in that wagon?" Thomas asked.

"No problem," the doctor replied. "We'll just leave one of our lady Professor's shoe trunks behind."

CHAPTER FIFTY

Tuzigoot Ruin, New Mexico

"We have acquired hard target," Hess whispered into his field microphone.

"Roger that. Acquire your soft target," Darstow instructed.

Hess surveyed his team. "Crevel," he called into his mike.

The short and stocky Belgian sergeant looked up from his perch in a cluster of juniper bushes just below the colonel's position. Each of the men was outfitted with a standard communication headset.

"Fan out."

Using single-word commands, Crevel instructed the team to slowly descend the steep walls of the canyon surrounding the alien craft, which was plainly visible in the strengthening light. Inch-by-inch, the men crept toward the craft, their silenced weapons at the ready. Hess remained at his elevated post and checked the team's progress with his powerful Zeiss binoculars.

When the team was within five meters of the craft, they spread out in a crescent and held their positions under whatever cover they could find. Then one man actually crept up to the craft's hull and gingerly placed a flat magnetic pickup mike on its now shimmering skin.

"Tapped," Crevel spoke into his headset.

Hess activated the flat mike, and slowly increased the gain until the speaker being fed by the mike began crackling static.

After making several adjustments, he concluded no one was inside the alien craft. Since the AD had made it clear the craft could not be opened without Professor Marcus Aaron, they would wait for Aaron to return.

"Camp out," he directed into his headset. He watched with some pride as each team member gathered brush to further mask their positions. They were virtually invisible.

* * *

"This is utterly fantastic." Andrew exclaimed. They stood together in the center of the shuttle, whose walls were becoming increasingly transparent with the gathering light of dawn. Staring through the west wall, Andrew watched with a mixed sense of fascination and fear as Hess's men crept down ever so slowly around the shuttle, completely oblivious that they were being observed by the shuttle's inhabitants. "You mean to tell me they cannot see us?"

"The shuttle's walls only allow external light and sound to enter, operating on a principal similar to one-way glass," Marcus explained. "Except of course, the shuttle's walls are made of a super-hard metal, not glass, and there are mechanisms in place to cut off the external light source altogether, if desired."

The journalist's considerable bulk took up much of the free space in the shuttle, and Marcus was beginning to feel a bit claustrophobic. He wiped his brow with his left sleeve.

"Let's go over it again, if you please."

Andrew nodded. "Exactly twenty-five minutes after you leave, I hit this switch." He pointed to a blue icon on a console just beneath his protruding stomach.

"You don't hit it," Marcus barked irritably. "You gently, but firmly, touch it."

"Fine, I'll touch it," Andrew said, with considerable indignation.

Marcus nodded his approval. "You must be careful not to touch anything else. I mean anything, until I return with my daughter. Do you understand?"

"I won't, I assure you."

A few moments passed.

"But what could happen if I, er…well, accidentally touch one of the other controls?"

"You might send this shuttle hurtling into space. And since you do not know how to guide it, it is unlikely you will ever manage to return." Marcus fixed his eyes on the journalist's imposing girth. "Actually, I imagine you would die of starvation, before anything else."

The admonition caused Andrew's ample stomach to rumble.

CHAPTER FIFTY-ONE

To Tuzigoot Ruin, New Mexico

Every time they hit another rut in the road, Mariah's heart skipped a beat.

"You needn't worry, my dear," Darstow said, in an almost soothing voice. He was seated in the front passenger seat, immediately in front of Mariah, who was lodged in the van's back seat separated from Brittany by Agent Russo.

"The charge around your daughter's fragile neck will not ignite unless I depress the red button on my transmitter." He withdrew the transmitter from his pocket and held his thumb over the button, like the *Sword of Damocles*. As he sensed Mariah's increasing fear, he caressed the button's surface, plainly relishing in her distress.

"You are such an animal," Mariah sobbed.

Darstow laughed. "You are so wrong, my dear. I am a hero. I am the man that is about to give our nation an incomparable military advantage over our enemies, both foreign and domestic. There is little the President and Congress will not do to reward me for my efforts."

"We're here," said Agent Leland, who was driving.

Darstow nodded, stuffed the transmitter back into his coat pocket, and exited the van as soon as it stopped. "Everybody out and into the jeep," he commanded.

The ride up the mesa's steep slope was rough, and several times Mariah thought she would be pitched out onto the dirt.

Throughout, Brittany had been stoic, afraid that if she made any sudden moves, the explosive charge encircling her neck would detonate.

At last, they reached the summit. Much of the open space was comprised of low foundations intersecting one another at odd angles. One part of the ruin was higher than the others, perched atop a knoll dotted with juniper scrub and Santa Rita prickly pear. A small stone building crowned the knoll, its facade covered with strange, seemingly ancient symbols. Mariah's heart raced. She recognized one of the symbols, the glyph to the far right of the others, at the cornerstone under the roof.

There was no doubt about it -- it was definitely the Sign Dad had traced for her so many years before. He had said he had created it just for her.

"It's time we had our little family reunion, don't you think?" Darstow whispered sarcastically. He gestured for Mariah to step out of the jeep. Russo gripped Brittany under both arms and lifted her out of the jeep's tiny rear compartment. The child's hands were still handcuffed behind her, although Mariah's handcuffs had been removed.

"What do you want me to do?" Mariah asked.

"Your father is below us, in that meadow." Darstow pointed beyond the ruin to the east, where a line of cottonwood trees spired out of a grassy valley.

Mariah nodded.

"He is hiding in an alien spacecraft he stole from us three years ago."

Mariah looked at Darstow as if he were mad.

Darstow ignored Mariah's incredulous stare, continuing, "You will go down to the meadow and find the spacecraft. You will draw your father out of the spacecraft, and bring him to me. And you will do all this within thirty minutes."

"And if I can't find the ship, or I do find it but Dad won't leave it, or for some reason, we don't get back in thirty minutes, you'll push that button?"

"Without hesitation. And then I'll kill you and incinerate the spacecraft, rather than let it slip through my fingers again."

"What assurance do I have that you will let Brittany live if my father returns with me?"

"None, really. But I would like your father to cooperate with us. I think I can best obtain that cooperation if you and your daughter are alive and…well, enjoying my protection." His voice lowered.

"Your choices are clear cut," he snapped. "Do as I say, and your family continues to breathe. Cross me, and I will kill you all. Which will it be?" He withdrew the transmitter from his pocket and placed his thumb on the detonator switch. Instinctively, Russo stepped away from Brittany, hoping to avoid the blast that might envelope her.

It was Russo's movement that convinced Mariah that Darstow was serious. "You said thirty minutes?"

Darstow pocketed the transmitter and glanced at his digital wristwatch. "It's seven thirty-five now. I'll expect you no later than eight o'five."

He winked at Mariah, as if they were two old friends. "Do try not to be late."

CHAPTER FIFTY-TWO

Tuzigoot Ruin, New Mexico

Marcus's greatest fear was getting shot by a surprised, trigger-happy soldier. But there was no profit in agonizing over the risks involved. He had spent months manipulating the parties to converge on this lonely mesa, and now was not the time to have second thoughts. His only hope was that Darstow had made the effort to use seasoned professionals.

Marcus took a deep breath, passed his hand over a series of photocells above the main hatchway, and the wall before him silently drew open. He quickly stepped outside, and the hatch instantly slid shut as soon as he cleared the threshold.

It was going to be a fine morning. A few puffy clouds were bunched together in the lightening blue of the eastern sky. The temperature felt about fifty degrees. Slowly, he climbed toward the main ruin, careful to keep his hands open and at his side so it was clear he was carrying no weapon.

"Stop. Or be shot." The order came from a megaphone, undoubtedly operated by one of the soldiers who had surrounded the shuttle.

Marcus immediately stopped and raised his hands. He tried not to move.

"On the ground, face first, with your hands at your head." the voice ordered.

Marcus fell to the ground to comply. Less than a minute later, he felt strong hands grip his arms and legs while others tightly handcuffed him. They lifted him to his feet where he faced several barrel-chested soldiers, each with an automatic rifle leveled at his torso.

Hess couldn't believe how easy it had been to capture the Professor. "Bird netted," he radioed Darstow, trying not to sound exultant.

"Deliver him, but keep the ship secured," the reply crackled back. "And watch for the girl. She's headed your way."

Hess motioned Crevel and two others to escort the Professor to Darstow's position at the ruins. He then commanded the rest of his team to hold their positions surrounding the spacecraft. He was glad to stay where he was. *What he wouldn't give to just spy the inside of that ship.*

* * *

It was Thomas's idea to skirt the main road up the mesa, to minimize the chances of their being detected. So grudgingly, they scaled the backside of the mesa, which was replete with sharply thorned trees and prickly cactus. They were often forced to backtrack when they ran into sheer walls preventing their ascent, but after more than three hours, they reached the summit, exhausted and bleeding.

"If I'd known the climb was going to be this demanding, I would never have agreed to take half this gear." Dov exclaimed, as he fell to the ground with a thud.

Trixie was so tired; she could only affirm Dov's comments with a frazzled glance.

Dr. Anthony and Thomas Kuzmic were having none of such talk, however. They had rushed over the summit to take up prone positions on the ledge overlooking the interior canyon of the mesa. Both fixed binoculars to their eyes.

"Do you see the group to the right of the ruin?" Anthony asked.

"Yea. Looks like the AD and his minions. And look there… a small girl. Look for Professor Aaron, or his spaceship," Thomas said.

"I'm still having a hard time believing that one." Anthony scanned the ground around the ruin, but could not detect anyone else, much less a flying saucer or rocket.

Thomas was about to quit his reconnaissance when he saw Mariah come into view, followed by three soldiers who were leading a bald, handcuffed man with a short black beard. "Bingo."

Anthony saw Mariah as well. "Is that the Professor and his daughter?"

Thomas didn't answer. "Dov, get your tired butt over here."

Dov pulled the glasses from Thomas and focused. "Looks like they came from the valley below the main ruin. I bet that's where the spaceship is situated."

Thomas nodded. "You're probably right. Now what the heck is our plan of action?"

Dov scratched his arm, a nervous habit he had developed when faced with seemingly insurmountable problems. "You know Darstow even better than I do. I bet he's got that spaceship ringed by an entire HRT squad, and there are probably at least five agents guarding his perimeter."

"Maybe two of us ought to try and find the spaceship, and the others follow the bad guy and his hostages," Anthony suggested.

Thomas shook his head. "We're so few, and up against so many, I think we should pick a primary target and stay with it." He looked around for support.

Dov and Trixie nodded their assent.

Dov fixed his gaze on Thomas. "We got into this because of Mariah. And both she and the Professor are being escorted to Darstow. That must mean he affixes especial significance to them. So I say stick to Mariah and her father like glue, and see where that takes us."

"Just like the old days," Thomas added. "You make the plan, and I execute it."

"Maybe you'll actually follow the plan this time," Dov said.

Thomas cocked his Uzi, grinning wickedly. "Hope springs eternal."

CHAPTER FIFTY-THREE

Tuzigoot Ruin, New Mexico

"Dad," Mariah hollered, as she saw her father round a bend in the trail she was descending into the canyon.

Marcus did not see her until he pinpointed the source of her cries. He began running toward her, only to be yanked to a halt by his guards.

Mariah rushed over and embraced him. "I missed you so much."

"I too," he said softly. He tried to nuzzle close to her, prevented from returning her embrace by his handcuffed hands.

"Dad, they've attached a bomb to Brittany, and they say they'll detonate it if you don't return the spaceship to them."

"I'll do what they ask, Mariah. I won't do anything to hurt Brittany."

Together, they trudged back up the trail towards Darstow's position, two soldiers ahead of them and three behind, all with automatic rifles at the ready. The canyon was completely silent except for the sound of their labored steps. After several minutes, they reached the crest of the trail.

"So Marcus, you thought you were rid of me, eh?" Darstow asked, as Marcus and Mariah walked the last few steps towards Darstow and his frail hostage.

"It's good to see you too, Keenan," Marcus muttered. "I'd hoped our next meeting would be at your funeral, but that nevertheless might be soon in any event."

"Such bravado from a handcuffed prisoner," Darstow jeered. "Perhaps you have one of your alien friends backing you up?"

Marcus just smiled. "Let my family go, Keenan. I'll turn the craft over, and instruct you on its operation, but I won't cooperate at all if you don't free Mariah and Brittany."

Darstow laughed. "I already have the ship, and I have you. To ensure your cooperation, I will hold the daughter and child until such time as you have told us everything you know about the ship and its creators."

"And what then, Keenan?" Marcus asked. "Are you really going to let the girls go, or are you just going to murder them like you did poor Henri?"

The accusation startled Mariah, and she fixed Marcus with an incredulous stare. "Murdered? He murdered Henri?"

"Don't believe the newspaper story you read about Henri being hit by a truck dear. Darstow shot Henri in the head as he attempted to board the ship with me in our effort to escape the air base with the craft. The poor man was dead in an instant. To cover up his crime, Darstow had the body incinerated, and concocted the story about Henri being burned in an accident with a fuel truck."

"You were both attempting to steal top secret government property," Darstow said. "I would have been justified in killing you both, if I could. You know, I might be able to finish the job sooner if you fail to cooperate to the letter."

Mariah lunged at Darstow's neck and attempted to throttle him. Agent Leland sprang to intercept her advance, but at that moment, the canyon was plunged into complete and utter darkness.

* * *

"What the heck?" Dov exclaimed.

"It's in the middle of the morning, for Chrissake," Thomas muttered. "Are we experiencing a total eclipse of the sun?"

They could see nothing. For one moment their eyes had been accustomed to the incredibly bright light of the New Mexico morning, and an instant later, the canyon had become blacker than the darkest cave.

"We'll have to feel our way to their position, pronto." Thomas said. With that, they rushed down from their lofty perch towards what they thought was the position of Darstow's party, experiencing severe cuts and bruises most of the way over the steep, cactus-riddled slope.

* * *

The instant darkness fell, Marcus turned toward Mariah and whispered desperately, "Lead us to the stone hut, the one with our special Sign at the top of the ridge just above us."

Mariah reached about and somehow managed to grasp Brittany, who had struggled out of Darstow's reach. Mariah grabbed Marcus by the arm and Brittany by her shoulder and led them in the direction of where she thought the stone building stood.

"Don't let them escape." Darstow screamed, unable to see anything in the pitch blackness.

"I can't see a damn thing," Agent Russo shouted.

"Well, get a flashlight," Darstow ordered.

In the confusion that followed the sudden onset of darkness, Mariah, Marcus, and Brittany managed to distance themselves from Darstow's party. "How do I know which way to head, Dad?" Mariah whispered in exasperated tones.

"You've always had an extraordinary sense of direction, honey," Marcus assured her. "Just get us to the stone hut, and I'll take it from there."

Darstow called out, "Marcus. Mariah. Come back or I'll detonate the girl's collar."

The threat stopped Mariah in her tracks. "He'll kill her Dad. We have to turn back."

Marcus had no opportunity to reply, for as suddenly as the sky had turned pitch black, the blinding light of day lit up the canyon like an acetylene torch.

* * *

It took a few seconds for Agent Leland's eyes to clear, but as soon as they did, he spied Mariah, Marcus, and Brittany on a ridge just to the right and above his position. He aimed his gun at Mariah, loosing two rounds that fell well short of their mark. It was his last act. Reacting to Leland's fire, Thomas had closed sufficient distance towards Leland to enable Thomas to empty most of his Uzi's entire magazine into Leland, cutting the G man nearly in half. Some of the HRT personnel who had regained their sight returned fire on Thomas's position, but they were quickly picked off by Anthony and Dov, who held superior covered positions on a ridge to the east and south. Upon drawing fire, Darstow and Russo ducked for cover behind one of the low walls of the ruin, but their handguns were little match for the firepower they were acquiring. Only two HRT men on the ridge with Darstow remained alive, and they were pinned down by alternating fire from Thomas, Dov, and Anthony, who was grinning madly from ear-to-ear as the barrel of his machine gun glowed red from the heat of the rounds speeding through it.

"If we can get to the stone building, I can prevent Darstow from hurting Brittany," Marcus pleaded, hoping Mariah would continue their race to the building. On instinct more than anything else, Mariah bolted toward the building with Brittany in tow. Marcus followed behind haltingly, for his handcuffs prevented him from using his hands for balance.

Trying to keep the Professor's company in view, while returning fire on enemy positions, had proven so much for Darstow that it was not until the Professor had nearly reached the stone hut that Darstow remembered that he held the detonator to the charge attached to Brittany's neck. He began shouting, over and over, "Hold your fire, or I'll detonate the bomb around the girl's neck."

Gradually, the canyon grew quiet. Darstow slowly stood and held the detonator aloft so all could see it.

"Trust me once again, Mariah," Marcus said, as they reached the threshold of the stone building, panting. "All detonators work on weak line of sight FM radio waves; once inside the stone hut, the waves won't be able to penetrate the walls to enable the bomb to detonate." The sincerity in his voice conveyed his confidence, and with that, Mariah leaped into the building with Brittany. Marcus followed close behind.

"Damn you to hell." Darstow screamed. He depressed the detonator button, as his thin lips curled into a wicked sneer.

CHAPTER FIFTY-FOUR

Tuzigoot Ruin, New Mexico

"What do we do now, Dad?" Mariah asked.

The stone building was a single, windowless room, the only light source being the doorway through which they had entered. While outside the building had appeared rectangular, inside it seemed as if one of the longer walls was a bit shorter than the other opposite. Upon entering the building, Marcus had removed the Maker encircling Brittany's neck and threw it outside. He then dove to the far intersection of the short wall and furiously dug into the loose dirt with his bound and bleeding hands.

"There, I've got them." he shouted, and motioned for Mariah and Brittany to join him.

"How are those going to help us?" Brittany asked. She pointed to the five small silver globes cradled in Marcus's hands.

"I hid these here last night," the Professor responded. "Didn't you understand the code on the key?" Not waiting for a response, he placed one of the globes in his mouth, and with some effort, swallowed the sphere. He urged Mariah and Brittany to each swallow one of the remaining spheres, which they did.

They heard a sound at the door and turned toward it. A soldier entered, his gun at the ready, and pointed directly at them. Incredibly, he appeared to fall out of focus, and then rushed toward them. They attempted to recoil away, but the room was far too small to avoid his advance. As he rushed into them, they felt nothing. The soldier appeared to have not felt them either, and he began cursing, although his speech was incredibly slowed, much like the sound on a tape recording that is played at a speed slower than appropriate.

The soldier yelled, "I can see you, dammit," as he thrashed about the room, trying to grab his frightened prey. He then drew his sidearm and began firing directly into them. Mariah screamed, but Marcus, Mariah, and Brittany were not injured. Instead, the bullets drove through them and ricocheted off the wall behind them, with one of the rounds striking the soldier in the knee. He screamed and fell down, cursing even more.

Marcus chuckled, trying to calm Mariah and Brittany. "While he can see us, he can't touch us, or hurt us in any way. We're now in a slightly different dimension than he, one that allows us to move about in his world, but not suffer the harms his world might want to visit upon us. But the time we have to enjoy the protection of this state is limited. We must return to the shuttle quickly."

With that, the Professor simply stepped through the soldier still thrashing about on the floor, and led Mariah and Brittany outside into the bright afternoon sun which, like all objects surrounding them, appeared a bit blurred.

They scrambled down from the building to the flat perch where Darstow, Russo and the one remaining soldier were crouched behind ruin walls, exchanging fire with Dov, Thomas, and Anthony. With Brittany in front of him, and Mariah behind, Marcus strode directly up to Darstow, seemingly oblivious to the gunfire from either side.

Darstow couldn't understand why Brittany was still alive. He leveled his gun at Mariah, threatening in an eerie, slow drone, "I'll kill her if you don't tell your forces to cease firing."

"You can't harm us, Keenan," Marcus said. "As for our friends," he gestured toward Dov's position, "I don't know who they are, but they certainly have our thanks."

Marcus marched Mariah and Brittany away from Darstow down the trail towards the shuttle.

"Turning to Russo, Darstow commanded, "Shoot the daughter." As Mariah made a futile attempt to hide, Russo fired twice into her, but the rounds appeared to go through her without effect. Russo emptied his gun into Mariah as she fled down the trail with Marcus and Brittany.

Darstow and his group tried to follow, but immediately came under suppressing fire from Thomas, Dov, and Anthony, who pinned them to their positions. Darstow grabbed his handheld radio and signaled Colonel Hess.

"Hess here. Do you need assistance?"

"The Professor, his daughter, and granddaughter are heading your way, but they are somehow impervious to bullets or any effort to apprehend them. See what you can do to stop them."

"Crevel, you and Buck net them when they pass by your positions," Hess ordered into his head mike.

Special Agents Crevel and Buck sprang into action. Buck unfurled a long green net from one of the many pockets in his backpack. Crevel ran up the trail to reconnoiter the targets. As the Professor and his party jogged past Buck's position, he threw the net over them as Crevel ran into them in an effort to knock them over. The soldiers' efforts were useless, however.

The Professor, Mariah, and Brittany strode through the net and Crevel without effort, and reached the shuttle with the frustrated soldiers trailing immediately behind.

As they approached the shuttle, the blurring between their dimension and that of the soldiers became less pronounced.

"It's wearing off." Marcus hissed. As he passed his hands in sequence over the photo cells that keyed the opening of the shuttle access hatch, Crevel's hands, which had been desperately attempting to grab the Professor, suddenly obtained purchase, and the Professor felt himself pulled away from the shuttle as the hatch raced open. Mariah and Brittany hurled themselves inside, surprised to see Sawyer, who had witnessed everything through the shuttle's transparent skin.

"Do something." Mariah shouted to Sawyer, but the journalist was frozen with fear, and in any event, had little room to maneuver around Brittany and Mariah to reach the door. The dimensional shift was no longer effective for Brittany. She seized a large, wrench-like object hanging from a peg on the east interior wall of the ship and ran outside to her grandfather, waving the wrench wildly in an effort to scare off Crevel and Buck, who were attempting to wrestle the Professor to the ground as he flashed from his altered dimension to their dimension every few seconds.

"Marcus."

The voice was female and came from a clearing immediately behind the Professor and his grappling attackers.

As Crevel turned toward the voice, Brittany managed to hit him in the head forcefully with the wrench. Crevel fell unconscious, but Buck continued to struggle with the Professor.

A shot rang out. Buck bled heavily from the abdomen and recoiled away from the Professor. As Marcus struggled up towards the ship, motioning Brittany inside, a rein of bullets poured down on them from Hess's team, which was positioned above them in a semi-circle to their left. One round struck Marcus in the fleshy part of his right side above his waist, spinning him into the shuttle.

Marcus began slipping into shock. He had to close the shuttle door before any of Darstow's men attempted to enter. Fighting unconsciousness, he stood to pass his hand over the interior photocell keypad, but was knocked over as Trixie Pentov dove head-first through the hatch. Marcus managed to recover sufficiently to touch the cells necessary to close the hatch behind her. Waves of pain shot through his injured flank, and he fell unconscious to the floor.

"Is he dead?" Sawyer asked.

Trixie examined Marcus. "I think he was only grazed, thank God," she said, and ordered Sawyer to take off his shirt, which she used to bandage Marcus's wound.

Mariah cradled her father's head in her lap. "Is there any water in here?"

They looked everywhere but found none.

"Now what do we do?" Mariah asked of no one in particular.

"He told me not to touch anything." Sawyer said. "He said if we did, we might be sent into space without any hope of getting back."

Outside, Hess's team had encircled the shuttle. Mariah saw each of the soldiers clearly through the spaceship's transparent walls.

"They can't see us," Sawyer said, anticipating her thoughts. "The Professor said the ship's skin is like a one-way mirror."

One of the soldiers outside put his hand to his headset and issued orders into his mike. The entire squad began firing at the shuttle, whose terrified inhabitants ducked for cover. But the rounds simply bounced harmlessly off the ship.

"Okay, let's go with the heavy stuff," Hess ordered.

Two of the soldiers drew back about thirty paces and aimed what looked like bazookas or rocket launchers towards the shuttle.

Mariah had seen enough. "We're getting the hell out of here," she yelled, and started hitting icons on the various brightly-lit control panels before her.

"No!" Andrew screamed and grasped her arms in an effort to prevent her from touching the panels. Without warning and without a sound, the shuttle lurched to a forty-five degree angle and zoomed through the stratosphere at an incredible rate of speed, its now unconscious crew oblivious to its destination.

CHAPTER FIFTY-FIVE

Tuzigoot Ruin, New Mexico

"Did you see that?" Thomas exclaimed, as what looked like a reverse lightning bolt flashed from the base of the canyon into the sky.

"I bet that was the spaceship," Dov said. He was positioned behind a large boulder to the right.

"If the spaceship's gone, I imagine Mariah, her father, and the girl managed to escape in it," Anthony piped in.

Their suspicions were strengthened when what remained of Hess's team jogged up the trail to fortify Darstow's position. Seeing that the soldiers carried heavy weapons, including mortars and rocket launchers, Thomas ordered everyone into one of Darstow's cars, which were parked immediately below them.

"How are we going to start the damn thing?" Anthony asked.

"You evidently never grew up in Brooklyn," Thomas yelled above the din of machine gun fire blazing around them. Using the last magazine of his Uzi, Thomas blew out the radiator of the first jeep and then joined Dov and Anthony in the second. With one deft stroke, he broke off a plastic panel just below the ignition key on the steering wheel, pulled out the steel locking mechanism, ripped off a wire coupling, and touched together two exposed wires. The jeep started instantly.

They pulled away, and as they clutched into second gear, they heard the deep "Kthunk" of a round leaving a mortar tube.

They careened down the narrow road leading from the top of the mesa as the round exploded with a great crash to the left of the jeep and immediately below the stone building, destroying one of its walls.

It was only then they realized Trixie Pentov was not among them.

CHAPTER FIFTY-SIX

Low Earth Orbit

It was utterly silent in the shuttle when Mariah awoke, her forehead sporting a small bruise where she hit a control panel during the shuttle's unexpected launch. The rest of the group lay about the small cabin. She found Marcus, who was still unconscious, although he was making low moaning sounds. His makeshift bandage was soaked in blood, and Mariah worried that he would soon need a transfusion.

"Where do you think we are?" Trixie asked.

Sometime after the shuttle had launched, its skin had turned opaque so that its crew could no longer see outside its interior.

"I have no idea." She turned to Andrew Sawyer. "Can you make the walls transparent again?"

"I don't know," replied Andrew. He gestured to a series of icons in front of Trixie, who rubbed a bright red bruise on her cheek as she struggled to rise. "I think the good Professor touched one of these icons to make the skin transparent, but I'm not sure."

Mariah began touching the icons identified by Andrew, and while little happened immediately, eventually the skin of the ship melted away to reveal their location-- a large docking bay facility of some kind. Below them lay the depths of space; at their heads and all around the craft was a large room filled with strange machinery, and bathed in a comforting golden light.

"To quote one of your classic movie lines," Andrew said, "I don't think we're in Kansas anymore."

"I wish we could get Dad awake," Mariah said. "He would know what to do."

Andrew then remembered the Brighters Marcus had given him as proof for his story. Reaching into his pocket, he gave Mariah one, urging her to place it in the Professor's mouth, but not let him swallow it.

"What will this do?" she said, eying him with suspicion.

"Your father said these are a sort of alien creature which impart strength and good feelings. He said to place them under the tongue or near a heat lamp."

Out of options, Mariah placed the colored stone under her father's tongue, watching him carefully to see that he did not swallow it. Nothing happened for a few minutes. But then, quite suddenly, her father's eyes opened, he laughed aloud, and sat up.

Marcus reached into his mouth and extracted what looked like a bushy green caterpillar. To his delight, and Mariah's disgust, he placed the caterpillar on his wound, allowing the insect to bury into his ragged flesh.

"What are you doing?" Mariah exclaimed in horror.

"As Mr. Sawyer no doubt told you dear, this is a Brighter, an alien creature that will help heal my wound, give me strength, and most importantly, improve my attitude. The poor beast will not live long, however, and so we must get ourselves settled before I begin to weaken again."

With that, Marcus pulled himself up and deftly passed his hands over a series of icons throughout the shuttle. A hatch to their right slid open, and Marcus waved them through and out of the shuttle into the docking bay, where they stood in a cluster awaiting the Professor's instructions.

Using one hand to stem his bleeding, while waving his other about the room as if he were a tour guide, Marcus announced, "Ladies and gentleman, you are now in orbit far above Earth. We are in what science fiction writers would call a "Mother Ship" built by a greatly advanced race of aliens called the Deminians. The shuttle that we took to reach this Mother Ship is far smaller than the ship, which originally held three shuttles, but now, alas, has but two. The shuttles and Mother Ship were crewed by six Deminians, all of whom were injured or killed in an unfortunate collision of two shuttles in the summer of 1947 near Roswell, New Mexico.

"One of the shuttles was relatively undamaged in the collision, and it, together with its single surviving crewmember, was seized by the Army Air Corps shortly after the collision. The surviving Deminian died a few days later. The Mother Ship has been uninhabited ever since the collision, at least until I learned the secrets of the damaged shuttle, which quite by accident delivered me to the Mother Ship when I first entered the shuttle's threshold. I have lived here in the Mother Ship, off and on, for the past three years, learning the Deminians' language and culture, as well as some of the basics of their advanced technology. Any questions?"

Andrew piped in, "Don't suppose there is any steak and kidney pie in the fridge?"

CHAPTER FIFTY-SEVEN

Tuzigoot Ruin, New Mexico

They raced back to Anthony's station wagon. After transferring their gear to the wagon, they riddled the jeep's radiator with bullets, and then roared off towards Santa Fe, where they intended to drop off Anthony and switch vehicles on their way to Medicine Stone.

"By the time their air support arrives, we'll be long gone," Thomas said.

"Where could Trixie have gone?" Dov muttered.

"No use fretting about her," Thomas said. "There is no way we can go looking for her now, not with the amount of force facing us in that canyon."

"Maybe she linked up with the Professor," Dr. Anthony offered, as he drove at a speed never envisioned by General Motors.

"Let's hope for her sake that she did," Dov said. "I shudder to think what may happen to her if she were to fall into Darstow's hands."

CHAPTER FIFTY-EIGHT

Low Earth Orbit

They had spent four days in the Mother Ship, and despite all the wonders it contained, she could not wring any joy about being there, at least not without her son. She had been incredibly relieved to learn from Trixie that Jacob was in Old Vic's care at some godforsaken New Mexico lake called Medicine Stone. She was not altogether comfortable with Trixie's admonition that her boy was being protected by tame grizzly bears, and she desperately wanted to fly down to Medicine Stone to retrieve Jacob.

But they could do nothing until Marcus regained sufficient strength to pilot the shuttle to the lake. Until then, all she could do is wait and explore what could very well be her new home for the foreseeable future.

Marcus appeared at the doorway wearing a new shirt, not a robe as he had done the past four days. "I think I'm well enough to make a run for Jacob," he said.

"Let's go now," she replied.

"You can't come. To bring you would only give Darstow another opportunity to capture you again. Up here, you're totally safe. Besides, you need to be with Brittany."

"Trixie can take care of her."

"She needs to be with her mother, in case the worst happens. Trixie will have to stay not to care for Brittany but because without me, she is the only person capable of deciphering the codes necessary to keep this ship in operation. Only Andrew will accompany me. He does not want to remain here anyway."

Mariah knew it was little use to argue with her father. She turned toward the glass window, which looked out upon the vast expanse of interstellar space. At this orbit, the stars appeared incredibly bright, far brighter than the night sky appeared anywhere on Earth. "You like Trixie, don't you?" she whispered.

"Yes, I guess I do," Marcus said.

"I like her too. She would make a wonderful addition to our family."

"Let's hope that family will all be together again in a fortnight."

CHAPTER FIFTY-NINE

Santa Fe, New Mexico

When they reached Santa Fe, Dr. Anthony refused to leave. "You guys got me into this mess, and I intend to see it through to the end."

"That could very well mean your end, Doc," Thomas said.

"I'm prepared for that eventuality, and besides, you'll need me if you manage to get yourselves shot up."

"He's got a point," Dov said, who was woefully tired after driving the last eighty miles of their journey.

After making a quick pit stop at Anthony's office, where they loaded up a number of medical supplies, and stopping again at Anthony's home, where they refreshed their ammunition from his remarkably vast private arsenal, the men gassed up the wagon and headed straight for Medicine Stone.

It was the dead of night when they reached the lodge. There were no lights on in the main lodge, and no cars in the drive. Thomas quietly got out of the car, instructing Dov and Anthony to remain inside with the doors locked. Dov, for one, was not eager to greet the bears after his initial encounter with them, but Anthony had a macabre fascination with the thought he could actually pet a grizzly without losing numerous body parts.

Thomas returned in a few minutes. "They've gone to the island. Even took the bears."

"What island?" Anthony asked.

"Medicine Stone is about thirty miles in diameter, and spotted with scores of islands. One of the smaller islands towards the far end of the lake is called Leonard Island. Although it appears small at the surface, it's riddled with underground caves. Some were inhabited by the Anasazi Indians thousands of years ago. Their petroglyphs are everywhere. That's where we'll find them."

"How do you know they're at Leonard?" Dov asked.

"Vic left a note for me that said his allergies were bothering him and that he had gone into town with the boy to see a doctor. The old man hasn't seen a doctor for twenty years. Whenever his allergies bother him, he heads off to Leonard and stays in one of the caves for a few days. Hell, he has all the comforts of home there; even has a Lazy Boy near an air shaft that he turned into a makeshift fireplace."

"Well, how do we get to Leonard?" Anthony asked.

"That's no problem so long as Vic left a boat and motor. You two wait in the lodge. I'll scoot down to the boathouse and take a look."

Dov was showing Anthony where Mentol had been feasted upon by Waldo when Thomas returned. "We're in luck. There's a single skiff left with a Johnson 25 all gassed up and ready."

They spent the better part of the next hour transferring as much of their gear as possible into the skiff. They then hid the car behind a thick stand of cottonwoods behind the barn.

The gunnels of the boat almost touched the waterline when Thomas joined Dr. Anthony and Dov in the boat. "Better hope we don't encounter any weather; we'll sink for sure." With that, he yanked the motor to life. They were guided only by the bright moonlight shining over the still water.

* * *

"Director Darstow?" the technician reported.

"Yes, what is it?" Darstow asked.

"The infrared satellites that you tasked to monitor the area around Medicine Stone Lake, in New Mexico, are showing some activity."

CHAPTER SIXTY

Low Earth Orbit

"The only way I can ever return, Andrew, assuming I survive my cancer, is to make certain that your story about what you've witnessed here is believed by the major media." Marcus handed Andrew a box full of what looked like small CDs. "To help you convince them this is no hoax, I've loaded these discs with a significant amount of data from this ship's main computer banks, all translated into English, and using Arabic numerals. The information contained on the discs is revolutionary science, and will instantly lend credibility to your story."

Marcus walked over to a low shelf running the length of the ship's enormous main viewing port, and retrieved a larger disc. He handed it to Andrew. "I've also prepared this video, which pictures much of the ship and shuttle, and contains a four-hour lecture by me on Deminian culture, politics, and technology, as well as how the shuttle fell into our government's hands.

"Finally, the video disc details my story, how Darstow killed my son-in-law and ransomed my grandchildren, all for no purpose other than to reverse design technology that once possessed, would enable America, and perhaps Darstow himself, to dominate the world."

"America already dominates the world," Andrew noted. "And frankly, that's okay with most of the western powers, at least."

"She does so with some effort and diplomacy," Marcus responded, "because there are at least a few nations with the capability of threatening her in some way. If America was so strong that all nations feared offending her in the slightest, she would soon cease to be America the beautiful and would become America the loathed. And that is especially true if someone like Darstow was leading the charge. Think about it."

Andrew slowly nodded his assent.

"What are your plans once you have Jacob?"

"That largely depends on Jacob and Mariah."

* * *

Mariah had discovered the small closet in the shuttle when she had searched for water while trapped in the vehicle. As Andrew and Marcus conferred down the hall, she slipped past them undetected into the shuttle and hid in the small closet. Jacob needed her and no one, not even her father, was going to prevent her from joining the effort to get her boy back.

CHAPTER SIXTY-ONE

Leonard Island, New Mexico

"I hope you know where you're going," Dov moaned, as he tried to follow Thomas and Dr. Anthony through the thick undergrowth of Leonard Island. They were each loaded down with at least sixty pounds of gear, mostly guns and ammunition, and the awkward loads, coupled with the dark of the night and unfamiliar terrain, made progress toward the caves difficult.

"Stop complaining and look for booby traps," Thomas cautioned them. "Old Vic will have set quite a few to discourage visitors."

"What kind of booby traps?" Anthony asked.

"Leg snares, pungi sticks, claymores for all I know."

"Holy Toledo," Anthony gasped, and drew himself back well behind Thomas. "I'm glad you're on point."

They crossed over a forty-foot high berm that seemed to ring the outer edge of the island and then gradually descended a series of narrow, vine-strewn passages of jagged boulders that eventually fed into a sixty-foot high sheer rock face several hundred yards in length. A small stream ran into a cave at the eastern end of the rock face, and it was there that Thomas directed them.

Thomas commanded them to a halt immediately before entering the stream at the mouth of the cave. He reached into the streambed and slowly pulled up a semi-taut cord that appeared to run from inside the cave to something directly in front of the cave mouth. "What's that?" Dov asked.

"Doorbell," he said. "When tripped, the cord rings a bell to warn that someone's approaching."

Avoiding the cord, they proceeded into the cave by wading in the streambed, Thomas first, followed by Dov and Anthony. Before entering the cave, they donned helmets fitted with carbide lanterns, which emitted a bright glow for about five yards.

After perhaps a half-mile, they came to a precipice where the stream fell into what sounded like a huge dark cavern. Thomas tossed a magnesium flare into the cavern, and for a few seconds, the cavern's jagged outlines were revealed. "It looks like the only way to proceed is to drop down into the cavern, doesn't it?" Thomas asked.

"Certainly does," Dov replied with some trepidation.

"That's what Old Vic is counting on. The real way is there." He gestured to the far right wall at the top of the precipice, which appeared to be a dead end. On close inspection, however, a small trail that descended further into the cave began just below the wall; the trail could not be seen until one was virtually upon it.

They proceeded down the trail for about a half hour. Only a few bats clung to the walls and ceiling of the cave, and those seemed oblivious to their human visitors.

"You don't want to be going through this passage at dusk or dawn," Thomas said.

"Why's that? Anthony asked.

"Something called the '*Andrea Doria*' effect. The *Andrea Doria* was a cruise ship that sank after being rammed by another luxury liner. While the two ships could have detected one another if their captains had been using radar, they didn't bother to turn their radars on because they were convinced they knew all the hazards in the area."

"Of course, bats leave their caves at night to feed on insects, and return just before dawn. Although bats use radar to navigate, it requires some effort to employ their radar. So in familiar places, such as entering and exiting their cave, they don't bother turning on their radar. If you happen to be inside a cave when the bats are either leaving or entering, they end up crashing into you because their radar is not on until they're outside."

"So they're not actually attacking you; they're just surprised by your presence?" Dov asked.

"Absolutely." Thomas pressed on.

Dov noticed that it was becoming increasingly warmer, and he stopped for a moment to remove his thin leather jacket, letting Anthony pass him in the narrow passage. As he was stuffing the jacket into one of the side pockets of his pack, he thought he heard breathing. He tried to focus on the breathing, which seemed regular in pace although high-pitched, as if from a child.

The breathing seemed to come from a narrow shaft that intersected the trail to the right. He starred intently down the shaft, but could see nothing beyond the flickering light thrown from his carbide lantern. He dropped his pack and entered the shaft, which seemed to increasingly narrow as he proceeded through. Just as he reached the point where he could proceed no further, his lantern was snuffed out by a sharp draft from above. He didn't have sufficient room to relight the lamp. He remained perfectly still and allowed his eyes to adjust to the utter blackness of the shaft. The breathing seemed to intensify, but still he saw nothing. Not until the bright orange eyes were upon him.

CHAPTER SIXTY-TWO

Leonard Island, New Mexico

"This time there better not be any screw ups, Colonel," Darstow admonished him.

The remainder of Hess's team, together with Russo and Darstow, were en route to Leonard Island in a Blackhawk helicopter fitted with silent running gear.

Piter Mentol had reported Jacob's presence at the lake immediately before all further transmissions from Mentol had ceased. Since Mentol had failed to return from Medicine Stone Lake, Darstow suspected Mentol and his team had been killed there and that perhaps, Jacob was still secreted somewhere nearby. If Jacob was at the lake, Marcus Aaron might go there to retrieve him. As a result, Darstow had the lake under constant satellite surveillance since the fiasco at Tuzigoot, hoping Marcus Aaron or his daughter might arrive there and with them, the spaceship. His hunch showed promise, for Darstow's agents reported two people had taken a boat from the lodge at Medicine Stone to Leonard Island. No heat signatures registered for these people after they entered the island's interior, so he concluded they were hiding somewhere underground. It was likely one of them was Jacob Bourassa.

Darstow's assumptions were strengthened when, just a day after the shootout at Tuzigoot, three additional people took a boat from the lodge at Medicine Stone Lake to Leonard Island

and again, their heat signatures were lost when they entered the island's interior.

Darstow fixed Hess with a confident stare. "We'll have the ship and Aaron in custody before dawn."

* * *

Fifteen minutes passed before Thomas and Dr. Anthony noticed Dov wasn't trailing behind. "Stay here, Mike," Thomas instructed. "I'll head back to see if I can find Dov. If you don't see us within fifteen minutes, assume we're in trouble and come for us."

Anthony nodded, and Thomas headed back with deliberate speed. It wasn't long until he came upon Dov's pack adjacent to the intersecting shaft. Peering into the dark shaft, he repeatedly called out Dov's name.

No one responded.

"Dammit." He cupped his hands around his mouth and called into the shaft, "Dov are you in the shaft? Have you fallen into some crevasse?"

No one answered.

Thomas extracted a long nylon rope from his pack, set the pack down beside Dov's, and snaked into the shaft, the flames of his carbide lantern flickering wildly on the ever-narrowing walls. But he found no sign of Dov, and reached a point where it was impossible for him to go further.

"Where could he be?" Anthony asked upon Thomas's return.

"We don't have time to look further for him," Thomas lamented. "Let's press on, and hope we meet up with him further down the trail."

After another quarter hour, they entered a large chamber separated by a slow running stream. Several shafts led from the chamber. Thomas chose the furthest to the right, and that shaft emptied into a large cavern with a domed ceiling lit by strings of Christmas lights bolted to the wall. In the center of the room Old Vic sat buried in a recliner, his shotgun pointed in their general direction. To the right were Waldo and Boris, both exercised by their entrance until each recognized Thomas, at which point they calmed down, although they still seemed a bit apprehensive about Dr. Anthony.

Jacob was sleeping on a throw rug adjacent to a small fireplace cut into the far wall. A cooler filled with Stroh's longnecks and corn dogs was shoved in a corner next to a small battery and gas generator supplying the power for the lights and the refrigerator.

"'Bout time you got here," Old Vic snapped. "What the hell happened?"

Thomas introduced Dr. Anthony and related all that had occurred to date. "What did you do with Mentol?"

Vic hesitated. "Funny that. We had him tied up purty good. No way could he have gotten away, especially since his wounds from Waldo were pretty bad. But one night we come home from fishing and dammit if he isn't gone altogether. Don't know where he could be, especially since he must a hoofed it and didn't take anything with him as far as I could see."

Thomas ruminated about Mentol being on the loose. "The man is dangerous, even if unarmed and wounded."

"We've somehow got to get the boy to his mother and grandfather before Darstow gets a hold of him," Anthony said. "Any ideas?"

Old Vic scratched his week-old stubble. "Well, if what you say about the grandfather is true, then I bet the grandfather will be coming here to get the boy. Hell, we don't need to do nothing but wait for his move."

"But the grandfather is only going to know about Medicine Stone Lake if Trixie Pentov hooked up with him and told him about your care of Jacob," Dr. Anthony said, nodding at Old Vic. "And we have no proof that occurred."

Warming to his theme, Anthony continued, "Even if Trixie told the grandfather about your safekeeping of the boy, how would he know to retrieve him in the caves on this island?"

"How about this," Thomas offered. "Vic, you and Dr. Anthony stay here with Jacob. I'll surveille the lodge for a few days and see who turns up. If the grandfather shows, I'll lead him here. If the bad guys show, I'll do my best to warn you if they look like they're headed to the island. If they get by me, you'll have to do your best to out run them."

They agreed that Thomas's suggestion made sense, and it was decided that he would head back to the lodge in the early morning.

Time was not on their side.

CHAPTER SIXTY-THREE

Leonard Island, New Mexico

They were all short albinos, with iridescent orange eyes and black, straight hair. Their lack of skin color made sense, given the fact their tribe had evidently lived in these caves for years, perhaps millennia. When Dov had seen the first, he had been so frightened that he had forgotten there was limited headroom in the narrow shaft and had unthinkingly stood to run, hitting his head on the ceiling so violently that he had briefly passed out.

When he awoke, he was in another part of the cave, lying on top of what looked like a crude stretcher. Many of them stood over him, more out of curiosity than fear or loathing. As time passed and a few of the children had offered him some sort of dried meat, he began to believe the primitive people would cause him no harm.

After his head cleared, he stood, carefully, to get a better idea of his surroundings. He was in a vast chamber, the walls of which were lined on three sides by what looked like adobe cliff dwellings similar to those used by the inhabitants of the Taos Pueblo. At the center of the chamber was a large fire pit that lit the entire chamber, over which was suspended a huge clay chimney resting on four legs that vented to the ceiling. All about him were half-naked children and a few women, although each of these was fully clothed in what looked like fur blankets, their long hair braided and curled at the ears like rams horns. The air smelled like a mixture of dried meat and fish. He saw no filth, nor any indication that these people had access to modern tools or technology.

"Does anyone speak English?" Dov offered, peering around the chamber.

His inquiry sparked a loud chorus of replies, none of which he could understand.

After a few minutes, a woman wrapped in a colorful blanket approached him. From her bearing and colorful clothing, she appeared to be a leader of some sort. She held a large polished wooden board in her hand, and waved him to her side. Setting the board on the ground, she sprinkled it with fine sand, and using a thin stick, drew a crude picture of a man, a boy and two large bears to one side of the board. At the other end she drew one man, and with that, searched Dov's eyes to see if he understood.

Dov nodded and gestured first to his chest, and then to the drawing of the single man. Then, using his index finger, he drew an arrow connecting the picture of the single man with the depiction of Vic, the bears, and the boy. The woman then drew another single man at the center of the board. Dov shrugged. The woman seemed to understand, abruptly turned and left.

The woman soon returned with an injured tribesman who was bleeding heavily from what looked like a puncture wound at his shoulder. Occasionally, the man would sop up the blood oozing from the wound with a grey cloth. Although obviously in great pain, the wounded man looked steadily at Dov, and then shook his head. The woman then helped him to the floor, where he was attended by several young boys who sprang forward from the crowd. The woman then pointed at Dov and clapped her hands.

A teenage boy wrapped in a fur blanket stepped forward and led Dov by the hand to a small, poorly lit adobe chamber accessed by a thick, wooden door. The chamber had an overwhelmingly rotten, acrid smell. The boy left Dov in the chamber and closed the door behind him. Dov wished he had his pack, which held glow sticks as well as a flashlight.

It took Dov's eyes several minutes to adjust to the low light. As he crossed the room to see if there was a door at its opposite end, he tripped over something and fell crashing to the ground.

"What the hell?" he fumed, dusting himself off. He examined the floor closely. To his horror, he had tripped over Piter Mentol.

Actually, he had tripped over Mentol's head, which had been severed from his body, and was still spinning around the rocky floor like a bloody top.

CHAPTER SIXTY-FOUR

Medicine Stone Lake, New Mexico

Since she was shut up in the cramped closet, she could not observe the shuttle's descent to Earth, although she certainly felt an increase in G forces as they rocketed to the surface. At times, she thought she could hear her father and Andrew Sawyer speaking, but their conversations were muffled. After about thirty minutes, she felt the shuttle lurch, as if it had landed on solid ground and then shifted. Again, she heard her father's voice, and it was then that she chose to make her appearance.

"What are you doing here?" the Professor roared, as Mariah popped into view from her cramped quarters.

"I'm here now, and I won't go back." she responded icily, facing him with her hands on her hips, looking defiant.

Marcus bit his lip, and looked at his watch, a Rolex Submariner that his wife had given him as an anniversary present just before her death. "You've really tested me this time, Mariah," he said bitterly. "But we only have two hours of bottled oxygen and may not be able to return to space for a significant period after we exit the ship, unless we want to risk nitrogen narcosis, so we're stuck with you, I'm afraid."

Mariah asked, "What's this about nitrogen narcosis? And why do we need bottled oxygen?"

The Professor touched an icon on one of the control panels and the skin of the shuttle dissolved to reveal that they were not on land, but instead, deep underwater. Bright lights from the exterior of the shuttle illuminated the surrounding depths, which drew schools of large fish.

"When the Deminians first visited our planet thousands of years ago, they built numerous bases, most of which were situated underwater, so as to hide their presence from the native peoples of the period. Remarkably, one of these bases is at the bottom of Medicine Stone Lake."

Marcus gestured towards the control panel before him. "I've known of this base for several years, and thought it best to land here instead of the lodge for obvious security reasons."

"Well, how do we get out of the shuttle and back on land?" Mariah queried.

"That's the rub, you see," the Professor responded. "Each base can usually be accessed directly from the shuttle through a series of large air locks connected to underground tunnels lying below the lake or ocean floor. These tunnels will lead both to the mainland as well as several caves on islands in the lake."

"But since this particular base may not have been accessed for over two thousand years, the air lock mechanisms allowing us to go directly to the tunnels from the shuttle may be jammed from lack of use. And that means we can only get to the tunnels by donning scuba gear and accessing the emergency air lock adjacent to the main tunnel docking bay, which operates on a simple hydraulic system rather than an electrical system like the main airlock."

Marcus continued, "It takes at least two people to access the emergency air lock. Even that may not work, and then we'll be forced to surface the shuttle and land it somewhere on land, a decidedly riskier proposition, given the fact Darstow and his army may be about."

Mariah said, "I've never had any scuba training. What's this nitrogen narcosis that you mentioned?"

"If we have to access the tunnels by donning scuba gear and entering through the emergency air lock, our bodies will begin to absorb nitrogen gas at an alarming rate, due to our severe depth. If we fail to pass through the emergency air lock within seven minutes, we need to decompress, that is, make stops at various higher depths, before we can proceed all the way to the surface."

"If we fail to do this, we will get what mariner's call the "Bends," which is a condition where nitrogen bubbles form in our bloodstream and lodge in our joints or brain, causing horrible pain, or even death, within seconds. You can see the same phenomenon if you shake a bottle of soda pop. If you shake it but not open it, it does not foam unduly. But, if you shake it and then open it immediately, rather than letting it sit for a while to permit the gas to disperse, the pop will foam up and out of the bottle. In our case, if we don't decompress as required, the nitrogen bubbles will foam out of our blood, lodge in our joints and brain, and kill us."

The Professor paused. "Glad you came?"

Mariah smiled weakly.

"To make matters worse, my dear, we only have two sets of scuba gear. Knowing we might have the opportunity to land underwater, we originally planned on a full tank for me, half a tank for Andrew here and the remaining half a tank for Jacob on the return, what with Andrew staying on to write his story. Now, if all three of us have to access the emergency air lock, you'll have to share one with me, which will reduce the amount of bottled oxygen in one of the tanks by half. And at this depth, an hour of oxygen at the surface only lasts thirty minutes, at best."

Andrew cut in, "I've got a thought, Professor. Assuming we can't access the tunnels directly from the shuttle without getting wet, why doesn't Mariah stay here, and you and I will swim through the emergency air lock and then open up the main access door to the shuttle from inside the tunnel? Then Mariah can join us through the direct route without having to swim at all."

Marcus brightened but quickly frowned. "That's a good plan, Andy," he said. "But unfortunately, we can't rely on it because the direct access mechanism may not work even if activated from inside the tunnel. If that's the case, we won't have sufficient oxygen to retrieve Jacob if one of us has to return to pick up Mariah and then return through the emergency air lock. The only answer is that Mariah will have to stay."

"Bullshit," Mariah screamed. Grabbing the same wrench Brittany had used to ward off the Professor's attackers at Tuzigoot, she hit Sawyer over the head with as much force as she could muster. Andrew's eyes fell into his forehead, and he passed out at her feet.

She glowered at her father. "If you think Andrew's story is more important than me retrieving Jacob, you're sorely mistaken."

CHAPTER SIXTY-FIVE

Leonard Island, New Mexico

"Find the cave access as soon as possible," Darstow barked into his head mike. With that, Hess's team rappelled from the helicopter to Leonard Island. As soon as the last man touched down, the team fanned out at fifty-meter intervals, and headed into the thick undergrowth. Each man wore night vision gear.

It took several hours before they discovered the cave mouth. Carefully stepping into the icy stream, they made their way into the inky depths of the cave, trying to use the gentle gurgling of the stream to mask the sound of their movements.

* * *

As Thomas readied his gear for his return to the lodge, a tiny bell sounded.

Thomas glanced at Old Vic. Nodding, the old man announced, "Somebody's at the door boys. Let's hope they can't find us, for I 'magine they're far better equipped than us."

"But you know this cave system like the back of your hand, right?" Anthony asked, hopefully. "If it's Darstow rather than the Professor, can't we just out run them?"

Old Vic shook his head. "I wish that were true. As far as I c'n tell, this is as far as we can go. If they get to this chamber, this is going to be where we make our last stand."

Boris yawned loudly, and that led Waldo to do the same. "Do you think they know about the bears?" Anthony asked.

"I hope not," Old Vic replied. "Besides, I haven't fed 'em for three days. Maybe any unwelcome visitors will seem more like appetizers than honored guests."

* * *

"Let me out of here." Dov yelled, over and over as he pounded on the rough-hewn door to the dark chamber.

His cries had largely been ignored for the better part of an hour. Finally, the door opened to reveal the same boy that had led him into the chamber. This time, however, the boy had a small bow slung over his shoulders, and a quiver on his back of what looked like wooden arrows topped with desiccated white mice. The boy motioned Dov to follow him through an ever narrowing passage. After a few minutes, the passage became so narrow Dov could only proceed by crawling forward on his elbows. As the opening narrowed to such an extent that he could only snake through it, he became seized with an overwhelming fear of being stuck, or worse, that a small seismic movement of the earth above him would cause him to be crushed like a bug. He started to sweat heavily, his fear crippling him from being able to proceed further.

"I can't go on," he yelped, and tried to back out. To his surprise, he couldn't move backwards at all, for the elevation of the passage was significantly higher to the rear than in the front such that the narrowness of the passage, combined with gravity, prevented his retreat.

Dov started to panic, his psyche at a near-breaking point. But then he saw a tiny, flickering light ahead and below him at a distance of perhaps ninety feet. Mustering all his strength, he pulled himself toward the light, desperately hoping the light would not be extinguished.

The light soon proved to be a small torch held aloft by the boy, who stood in a large chamber into which the narrow passage emptied at a height of about seven feet. Dov dragged himself through the mouth of the narrow passage and fell thankfully to the floor of the larger chamber.

It was not until then, after his claustrophobia had subsided, that he noticed that other than what looked like a wood and stone altar of some sort placed at the chamber's center, nothing in the chamber appeared to be of primitive origin. Rather, the chamber was filled with strange, gleaming metallic equipment, some of which bore flashing green and maroon icons of a type he didn't recognize. At opposite walls were two large matte-black hatches, perhaps ten by twelve feet in size. Adjacent to the large hatch at the far end of the chamber was a much smaller hatch, about the size of a large refrigerator. And stranger still, that hatch appeared to be opening towards them.

CHAPTER SIXTY-SIX

Leonard Island, New Mexico

"Ninne vinne ya. Ninne vinne ya." The boy mouthed over and over, excitedly pointing to the opening hatch.

Dov looked at him blankly. The boy then took Dov's hand and forcibly led him to the primitive altar at the center of the chamber, where he motioned Dov to follow his example of laying prostrate before the altar. This was too much for Dov, and the best he could muster was to crouch behind the altar, attempting to conceal as much of his torso as possible behind the altar's aged center beam.

As the hatch swung open wider, the boy began chanting rhythmically, and at an ever increasing volume, "Atara demin patara donso." Dov implored him to be quiet, but the boy paid him no heed. Given the boy's incessant chanting, Dov had no illusions about being able to hide from whomever or whatever would be coming through the hatch, and the fact that he had no visible means of escape freed him to focus on the hatch as it steadily inched open before them.

As the hatch opened to an angle of 90 degrees, he saw that it formed the exit to a long hallway of chromed metal. At the end of the hallway, and approaching their position from about 100 feet, a four-legged, four-armed beast with two heads encased in glass and surrounded by thin tentacles trudged toward them. Gripped with a fear like nothing he had ever experienced, Dov crouched down under the altar, hoping it would conceal his bulk. His movements interrupted the boy's chanting for a sufficient amount of time for the boy to shoot Dov a disdainful glance, but he then continued his chanting at an even higher pitch.

Suddenly, the boy leaped up and over the altar. As Dov peered around the altar, what he thought was a two-headed monster were two scuba divers, the taller of the two a man, and the smaller a woman, sharing a single compressed air tank through some sort of octopus harness. He stood to get a better view as the divers strode through the hatch into the chamber, where they were greeted by the boy, who enthusiastically embraced the male diver around the right ankle.

"And what have we here," the male diver asked, as he removed his mask while simultaneously trying to unwind the boy from around his ankle. It was Marcus Aaron.

"Attapa benotoso demin pspta." The boy exclaimed.

Aaron starred a moment at the boy and replied, "Attapa demin satao psotos, akks bebenit."

The boy brightened, as if he understood Aaron perfectly, and then pointed to Dov, said, "Footssoto kherki altosooti?"

Aaron looked at Dov, and said, "Well, who might you be?"

"I'm one of your allies, Dr. Aaron. My name is Dov Bar-Lev. My friends and I were holding off Keenan Darstow and his agents at Tuzigoot while you and your daughter made your escape, although we still can't figure out how you did it."

As Dov spoke, the second diver removed her mask, and Dov instantly recognized her as Mariah Bourassa, Aaron's strikingly beautiful daughter. She was incredibly gorgeous, despite the fact that her long, blazing red hair lay in a soggy mass around her thin, alabaster neck.

The Professor smiled widely. "Ahh, the good Assistant Director Trixie told us so much about." Gesturing to Mariah, the Professor said, "May I introduce my *unmarried* daughter, Mariah."

Mariah snuck her father a dagger-like glance.

Undeterred, the Professor continued, "Mariah may need a friend in law enforcement since not ten minutes ago, she committed an assault and battery."

Having had enough, Mariah asked Dov, "Have you seen my son, Jacob?"

"Actually, I haven't seen him recently," Dov replied. He quickly related how they had left Jacob in the care of Old Vic, traveled to Leonard Island, and how Dov had been captured during the effort to retrieve the boy. Dov concluded, "I guess I'm the only one of the three that were captured by the Indians, and they led me to this room."

"It's fortunate that events unfolded as they did," Aaron smiled. He looked at the Indian boy and said, "Ddod dintosn paidi toquakute." The Professor grabbed the boy by the arm and led him to a corner, where they spoke in hushed tones. While they conversed, Dov caught himself glancing repeatedly at the shapely Mariah, who had removed her dive gear and attempted to dry herself off with a small towel she had retrieved from a watertight bag.

Embarrassed, yet flattered by the pudgy agent's hidden glances, Mariah asked, "Well, Agent Bar-Lev, how do we go about finding my son?"

"My friends call me Dov," he replied hopefully, but then grew more serious in tone. "I don't really know, Ms. Bourassa."

"Well, my friends call me Mariah, and so can you."

The Professor returned with the Indian boy, and they positioned themselves just below the narrow passage that emptied into the chamber. The Professor gestured towards Dov. "Give us a hand here, please," he urged. Together, Dov and the Professor boosted the boy back into the narrow passage, where he clambered inside and out of their view.

"Where's he going?" asked Mariah.

"He's going to see if the tribe's warrior clan can find and return Jacob to this chamber." The Professor pointed to the large hatch opposite the smaller one that the Professor and Mariah had entered. "We're going to try to find Jacob by proceeding through that interior access door, which according to our young Anasazi friend, is apparently a far easier route into the cave than the one you took to get here, Agent Bar-Lev. Our mission is to get Jacob back here and escape to the shuttle before your colleague Keenan Darstow makes his appearance."

"Wouldn't it be safer just to stay here?" Dov asked. "Surely the Indians can find Jacob faster than we can."

"Yes, but two eyes are better than one, and so rather than sit on our hands, we should do our part to find Jacob."

"Amen to that," Mariah chimed. "How do we get out of here?"

"First things first," the Professor said. He bent over a glowing control panel and touched a number of icons, all the while glancing intermittently at the large hatch next to the smaller one through which he and Mariah had entered. Slowly and silently, the larger hatch opened to reveal a long hallway, the walls of which were lined with gleaming chrome. The hallway appeared to incline gradually, and appeared to have a rubber-like floor.

"Yes!" the Professor exclaimed as the hatch swung open. "Mariah, you and Agent Bar-Lev stay here while I retrieve Andrew, assuming Mariah didn't kill him."

The Professor jogged into the open corridor and was gone for about twenty minutes. Eventually he returned with a short, corpulent man with a bandaged head who walked as if he had a hangover. The man looked at Mariah with some trepidation.

"What the bloody hell did you hit me for?" he said, glaring at Mariah.

"I wanted to see my son. I'm sorry I hit you. I truly am," she said as sweetly as she could muster.

The fat man gingerly touched his bandaged head, shivering with pain as his hands made contact with his bloody scalp. The Professor had already told Andrew about Dov, but Andrew felt an introduction was in order. Extending his hand, he said, "Andrew Sawyer, sir, a journalist soon to be on the masthead of the *London Times*."

Dov was impressed that the journalist was polite enough to go to the bother of making a formal introduction despite his injury, and taking Andrew's hand, responded, "Dov Bar-Lev, Assistant Director, FBI. But in view of what I've done to date, I'm likely to soon be out of work, if not in jail."

Andrew immediately took to Dov's self-effacing, genuine manner. Bar-Lev's counterpart at Scotland Yard would surely have talked down to Andrew, not treated him as an equal as this extraordinary young man had done.

Seizing Dov by both shoulders, Andrew said in a fatherly fashion while glancing at Mariah, "Be careful with this lass, Mr. Bar-Lev. When you least expect it, she'll conk your noggin."

"Let's hope there is no more noggin conking," Marcus Aaron said, as he again bent over a control panel and flashed his fingers over a number of colored icons. He turned toward the last unopened hatch, at the rear of the room. It silently swung open to reveal a dark passageway ringed with thick cobwebs.

Deeper inside, at its center, glowed two sets of unblinking, bright orange eyes.

CHAPTER SIXTY-SEVEN

Leonard Island, New Mexico

They arrived at the falls. "Looks like a bit of a rappel, eh," Sergeant Crevel said, peering over the edge of the raging torrent. His head was still bandaged where Brittany had hit him.

"Crevel, you and Preston scout the area to see if there is another route," Colonel Hess ordered, hoping they wouldn't have to descend into the dark cavern through the raging falls. "A soldier is never as exposed to enemy fire as when he is hanging by a rope," he said.

"Colonel, over here." Preston called. "I've located a hidden path at the far wall."

With relief, Hess's team proceeded down the narrowing passage in single file, the green glow of their night vision goggles occasionally flickering off the dew clinging to the rocky ceiling.

"Haooooo." The unintelligible scream had come from behind, but because there was no room to maneuver, it was impossible to see around the men immediately behind.

"Everybody down." Hess ordered. As best they could, the team crouched down, their weapons at ready and directed to the rear. Hess remained standing. He counted six men, other than himself. That was a problem.

A moment before, there had been seven.

* * *

"I think there's smoke coming up from that precipice," Russo said, pointing to a juniper encrusted ridge at the southern edge of the island.

"So there is," Darstow said. He ordered their helicopter, which was fitted with floats, to set down in the water adjacent to the ridge.

Loading Russo down with several hundred feet of rappelling line, Darstow led the agent up the ridge to the place where the smoke escaped. Sure enough, it looked as though a man could pass through the smoke belching passage. "Go back to the chopper and get the gas masks," Darstow commanded.

After Russo retrieved the masks, Darstow tied the rope to a large fir tree a few yards from the smoking passage. They dropped the line into the passage to see how far it fell. It seemed to fall completely down the shaft.

Darstow retrieved the line and tied the free end around his waist with a bow line. He then fitted a carbide lantern to his head, donned his gas mask, and instructed Russo to slowly lower him into the shaft. "If I pull several times, hard, pull me up."

Russo mouthed his acquiescence.

The shaft was really a series of remarkably aligned, narrow vertical passages occasionally interrupted by large, dank caverns so immense Darstow often could not see their surrounding walls. His vision was most impaired when he was in an especially narrow section of the shaft, and because his gas mask was stifling, he removed it and rested within the confines of every large cavern he encountered. Eventually, bone-tired and with hands bloodied from the ordeal of clinging to the rough line, he reached the floor of the shaft, where the balance of the line lay curled. He unfastened the line from around his waist and noticed a musty, almost feral smell. He followed it through a series of narrow horizontal passages tinged with a thin line of smoke, which hugged the upper reaches of the ceiling.

After what seemed like a half hour, he heard voices. Flushed with excitement, he plodded on through the dark passageway, all the while following the smoke trail and foul smell, which had grown stronger.

He soon came upon a bright light shining through a vertical passage intersecting his path. He peered down the shaft and saw a log fire about twelve feet below.

Darstow drew his SIG P229 .40 caliber semi-automatic and checked to ensure that a round was chambered. With his gun in his right hand, and his left hand pressing his hard hat to his head, he dropped down into the fire.

CHAPTER SIXTY-EIGHT

Leonard Island, New Mexico

As soon as Marcus and company entered the passage, the two Indians retreated, but not before hanging lighted torches along the passage, which on closer inspection appeared to be arrows tipped with desiccated white mice soaked in some sort of flammable liquid. As the mice burned, they emitted a smell similar to how hamburger might smell if fried in turpentine.

"That smell is just awful," Mariah coughed, as she passed by one of the torches.

"Just the same, it's nice of them to light the way, so to speak," Dov said, following close behind her.

The Professor had taken the lead, with Andrew Sawyer taking up the rear.

"Do you have a clue where you're going Dad?" Mariah shouted.

"Our friends are leading us where they want us to go. I just hope it's where we want to be," the Professor said.

The passage was certainly not naturally formed, for the walls, though made of solid limestone, were perfectly flat and of even diameter. The floor sloped upward at a steady three-percent grade, and they were all out of breath after twenty minutes.

"I've got to stop for a moment," Andrew fell to the floor in a heap.

"Me too," Mariah leaned against what she thought was the wall. But no wall was actually there, and she fell through the wall into a metal closet of some sort, which became brightly illuminated upon her entry.

"Eehhhh!" Mariah screamed as she banged her knee on a low cabinet at the threshold. Mariah struggled to her feet. She could see no doorway into the closet. Only white walls covered by metal cabinets of varying sizes. With some trepidation, she opened one of the lower cabinets. It contained a number of spacesuits, except they were extremely small, child-like in size. Other cabinets contained unfamiliar mechanical devices, although some looked as if they might be weapons, or even communication devices.

Dov burst through the wall and lurched into Mariah, sending them both careening into the far corner. He landed squarely on top of Mariah, who upon regaining her composure, said, with a giggle, "You could have knocked."

Embarrassed, but secretly thrilled to have such close contact with Mariah, Dov pulled himself to his feet and helped Mariah do the same. "I'm sorry. When I saw you fall through the wall, I started pressing the area where you disappeared, but nothing happened. Then Andrew came over and when he was immediately behind me, I fell through the wall too."

Mariah laughed. "I guess we should be glad you crashed into me rather than Andrew."

They both chuckled at that one.

"Well, what's all this?" Dov asked, as he gestured to the cabinets and their contents which Mariah had strewn about the floor.

"I imagine Dad would know. But how do we get out of here?"

Dov began shoving against the wall they had entered, but he was no more successful in opening an exit than Mariah.

"No offense, Dov, but if I'm going to be stuck in this little closet with you for an eternity, you're going to have to bathe."

"I imagine I'm pretty ripe," Dov acknowledged. "I'll try to keep my distance."

"At least until you take that bath," Mariah smiled.

Dov's heart soared.

Mariah opened more cabinets, as Dov shouted in the direction of the exit, "Andrew. Professor? Can you hear us? We're behind this wall, trapped."

They heard nothing. Then the wall opened to reveal Marcus and Andrew.

"Good job, kids," the Professor said.

He and Andrew crowded into the small closet, and upon their entry, the exit wall again disappeared.

"Well, I hope you know how to open that again," Mariah chided. "We've tried everything."

"But I do, you see." The Professor ground his right toes into a slight depression before the wall while pressing the wall with his hand. As he did so, the wall disappeared to reveal the passage.

"Amazing." was all Dov could mutter.

"We don't have much time to lose," Marcus said. He opened more cabinets and threw the contents of some into a pile at the far corner.

"What is this stuff, Dad?" Mariah asked.

"This is a sort of storage locker the Deminians have in each of their staging bases. You just happened to find it by dumb luck. I'm certainly grateful for that, for there are some things in here not found on the shuttle or even the ship, but may help us if we encounter Mr. Darstow and his gang."

The Professor pulled metallic belts out of one of the cabinets, and handed them to Andrew, Mariah, and Dov, fitting a fourth belt to his waist. The belt given Andrew was not large enough to circumnavigate his ample waist, so Marcus instructed him to wear it like a bandoleer.

"These belts emit a magnetic charge in a circular pattern that deflects projectiles, anything from arrow points to bullets," Marcus said. "But the charge is only designed to protect Deminians, who were never more than five feet tall. So most of us will be unprotected below our ankles, assuming we keep the belts above our waists."

"How do we turn them on?" Dov asked, feeling the belt to discover an "on/off" switch.

"Oh, that's easy," the Professor said, chuckling. "All you have to do is sing."

CHAPTER SIXTY-NINE

Leonard Island, New Mexico

Helpless to prevent further incursions from the rear in his present position, Colonel Hess ordered his team to double-time forward. They knew they were on the right track, for occasionally, they would spy the impression of a boot in some of the thicker mounds of bat guano that lined the floor of the cave.

At last, they rounded a bend and burst into a large chamber illuminated at the far end by a wood fire that burned so brightly they were temporarily blinded. Hess and his team tore off their night vision gear. The Colonel ordered the men to fan out. A recliner at the center of the chamber was still rocking, but they saw no sign of its recent inhabitant. Just as the Colonel's eyes began to adjust to the increased brightness of the chamber, he heard a crash at the fire.

Flaming logs flew out the bottom of the hearth, where a man in a gas mask with pants afire struggled to stand. The entire team trained its guns on the man, who cursed furiously as he attempted to pat out the flames that enveloped him.

"Damn it!" Darstow screamed, as he dropped his pistol, and rolled to the ground in an effort to extinguish the flames.

"Hold your fire." Hess hollered. "It's the AD." Hess ran to Darstow, his head low in case of sniper fire. He threw himself over Darstow to smother the flames.

"Get the hell off me." Darstow cried as he tossed the Colonel aside and sprang to his feet to retrieve his weapon. His pants smoldered. "Have you seen them?"

"Yes, I believe he has." The voice of an elderly man replied. He stood outside of the light spewed by the makeshift firepit. "Sic 'em Waldo."

A terrible bellow echoed off the chamber walls, and as Hess's team turned its attention on it, Boris pounced from their rear and ripped the head off the trailing man, clawing the man immediately in front so badly that he was instantly rendered unconscious from the shock attendant to a massive loss of blood. As the team turned toward Boris, Waldo joined the fray and lunged into the lead man, ripped his rifle from his hands, latched onto his right leg, and tore it clean away. Through it all, Thomas, Dr. Anthony, and Old Vic peppered those in the middle with shotgun and rifle fire.

Although hardened from numerous encounters with criminals and terrorists of every ilk, the assault by the grizzlies, coupled with the sniper fire, was too much for Hess's team. The three still alive and mobile bolted in a panic back through the entry passage, leaving most of their weapons, as well as Darstow and Hess, behind.

As soon as the bears attacked, Darstow and Hess took refuge behind the recliner. Each only had a semi-automatic pistol, which was clearly no match for the bears, let alone the shotgun and rifle fire being directed at them by their hidden adversaries. Darstow shot several times at Waldo, narrowly missing the bear in the darkened cavern.

"Don't shoot the bears." Hess shouted over the din. "You'll just make them mad, and then they'll come over here to finish us off."

Nodding, Darstow concentrated his shots in the direction of the rifle and shotgun fire. As it was, the recliner was well-shredded from shotgun blasts, and with each new round pummeling the chair, their cover diminished. When the action on his pistol locked open, signaling that his magazine was empty, Darstow realized his prospects were decidedly grim.

"Give up Darstow. If you throw down your guns, we'll prevent the bears from eating you." The voice was familiar to Darstow. *Who is that?*

"Our men will be back in a few minutes, and this time they'll be ready for your bears," Darstow shouted. His admonition lacked conviction, for as he spoke, Waldo and Boris gorged themselves on the carcasses of the three men they had felled. The sound of flesh being ripped from the torsos of the hapless soldiers sickened Darstow; when it became clear that the remnants of Hess's team were not coming to their rescue, he threw his now empty pistol to the floor, instructing Hess to do likewise.

With that, the rifle fire ceased. Slowly, Thomas, Anthony, and Old Vic approached. The bears continued to feed on their victims, oblivious to the five men at the center of the chamber.

"So it's you." Darstow spat at Thomas's feet. "I thought I recognized your voice. Kuzmic, right? The former SEAL, HRT leader?"

Hess recognized Thomas, and even smiled when he approached.

"Good to see you, Colonel," Thomas spoke to Hess, ignoring Darstow while keeping his Uzi trained on both men. "I'm sorry you're involved in this mess. I really have no beef with you. As far as I'm concerned, you're free to go."

"You know I can't leave the AD," Hess said.

"Yeah, I know." Thomas turned to Anthony. "Doctor, tie up the good Colonel. Good and tight, cause he's an expert at getting out of tight jams."

As Anthony complied, Thomas made eye contact with Darstow, and the older man flinched from the hatred emanating from the younger man's glance.

"Why have you got yourself involved in all this, Kuzmic?" Darstow asked. "This is a national security matter, and as you can see, it portends nothing but trouble for you, without profit."

"Well, you see, apart from you wrecking my house, I'm doing this for three reasons," Thomas whispered, beginning to circle Darstow like a boxer ready to strike."

"First, I'm doing this for Dov Bar-Lev, my friend."

Darstow snickered at the mention of Dov's name.

"Second," Thomas said, as he continued to encircle Darstow even faster, "I'm doing this because I want to prevent you from hurting Jacob Bourassa."

Darstow's lip curled in a snarl. "I assure you, I mean the boy no harm."

Thomas laughed at that. "And finally, you bastard, I'm doing this because you killed my Lisl with that stupid bombing in Beirut. And *that one* is the reason I'm going to kill you right now."

With that, Thomas dropped his Uzi to the side and threw himself into Darstow, raining the older man with lightning quick kicks and chops. Darstow fended off most of Thomas's initial blows until the men fell over the tattered recliner to the floor. There, each twisted, punched and kicked the other with frenzied zeal. Owing to his youth and fired by his rage, Thomas got the better licks in, and Darstow soon became fatigued.

Gripping Darstow's head in a headlock, Thomas bent the FBI man over his right knee, in an effort to snap the man's neck. Darstow screamed in agony and tried to pull his head free. Just as Thomas was about to deliver the *coup-de-grace*, Jacob approached out of the shadows, looking at him disapprovingly.

"Damn," Thomas exclaimed. He released his grip on Darstow, who fell to the floor from asphyxia. Thomas looked down at Darstow's spent frame. "It would be too easy for me to kill you, Darstow. No, the best punishment is for Dov to arrest you, and stick you in prison for all eternity for your crimes."

He tied Darstow's hands tightly as the older man lay prostrate at his feet. Turning to Old Vic, he asked, "Now what?"

"I reckon we ought to get the heck out a here. We can use these two as hostages if the other soldiers are wait'n to ambush us as we go out."

"But what about waiting for the boy's grandfather?" Thomas asked.

"I don't have no magic answer about that," Old Vic reflected. "Either he'll show up at the lodge, or he won't. But now that the element of surprise is gone, wouldn't it be better if we skedaddle from here?"

Anthony and Thomas slowly nodded their heads.

Thomas glanced at the bears, which were quietly continuing to feed. "What about those two?"

"Well, they'll eventually foller us out, after they've had their fill. Just stay wide of 'em." Old Vic chuckled, "Remember, never git between a dog and his bone, so to speak, especially one with foot-long claws."

Thomas and Anthony smiled weakly.

With Hess and Darstow at the lead, followed by Thomas, Jacob, Anthony, and then Old Vic, they carefully edged out of the chamber back into the entry passage without provoking a reaction by the bears, who had calmed considerably. They encountered no resistance from the retreating soldiers.

The albino cavemen, however, were an entirely different matter.

CHAPTER SEVENTY

Low Earth Orbit

"It's so beautiful here," isn't it dear?" Trixie asked.

Brittany said nothing and stared out the window into space.

"I know you miss them, but don't worry, they'll be back before you know it."

"I know they will," the girl muttered, irritably. "But when they do, I don't want to stay here, or go with grandpa to another planet. I want to go home and be with my friends."

Trixie said nothing.

"It's just that it's so quiet here," Brittany continued. "And there's nothing to do, at least nothing we understand. And there are no boys, and no girls, and no parties, and…no nothing."

"'Nothing,' dear, not 'no nothing.' Your grandfather would have a heart attack if he heard the way you talk sometimes," Trixie chided. "If he can speak grammatically perfect Navajo, you can certainly make an effort to speak proper English."

Brittany smiled, and turned again toward the window. "Can we have something to eat?"

Trixie made her way to the "kitchen," a large pantry off the main lobby replete with devices that apparently dispensed food, of sorts. The device Marcus had instructed her to use disgorged a sort of textured pudding that tasted like a cross between butterscotch and tapioca. Marcus had said it was the only food on the ship that people would find palatable, but Trixie had always judged Marcus's tastes pedestrian, and she was eager to try other foods that might be dispensed by the surrounding machines.

"I think we'll try something different for a change." She looked at the various machines and was drawn to one in particular, not only because it seemed larger than the others, but because it had a bright, emerald view screen of some sort at its center. A number of green and amber icons glowed at its base.

Trixie studied them for a while. She could not decipher the icons, however, and so she simply began pressing them in the same sequence as was necessary to get the 'pudding' dispenser to operate. But no pudding emerged. Instead, to her astonishment, the view screen turned from emerald to white, and then a small alien with large, kind eyes appeared on the screen.

"You are there," it said, but without words.

"How can you understand me?" she whispered, her curiosity overcoming her surprise.

The alien seemed to dismiss her inquiry as silly, and asked, "Where is Aaron?"

"He is on Earth trying to retrieve his grandson from the government men." This time, she thought the words rather than spoke them, and to her delight, the alien appeared to understand her perfectly.

"There is little time. The ship will return to us in only two more of your days. All who are not on board will be left."

"What do you mean 'left?'"

"Two days only. Thereafter, no more," the alien vanished as suddenly as he appeared.

CHAPTER SEVENTY-ONE

Leonard Island, New Mexico

Marcus glanced at his watch as they exited the storage locker. "We've got no time to lose." He ordered his companions to quicken their pace up the torch-lit passage. They jogged perhaps another quarter mile and abruptly halted at the entrance to yet another chamber, this one brightly lit by flaming torches and ringed by hundreds of dark haired, albino Indians similar in appearance and dress to the boy they had encountered in the docking bay. The chamber was completely silent. At its center stood a stately woman swathed in brightly colored robes, her hands held out in a gesture of friendship. To her right, lying on the ground face up but fully bound, were four soldiers dressed in SWAT battle gear. The soldiers were clearly frightened.

"Ialso psotkkeet, Birrlloostapa." The Indian woman spoke.

Marcus considered her statement, and replied, "Slol Ialso taparra Birrlloostapa, illin oyoa oyoa ta."

The woman smiled and gestured them to join her, clearly pleased with what she had heard.

"What did you say, Dad?" whispered Mariah as she smiled at the woman.

Marcus whispered, "They believe us to be the Deminians, who are part of their tribal lore. Our identity was confirmed first by our entrance through the docking bay, which they believe to be a sacred route to heaven, and by my ability to converse with them in Anasazi, their language."

Well, what about the soldiers?" Dov pointed to the men at the Indian woman's feet. "Why did they capture them, but leave us be?"

"They no doubt entered the cave complex through the usual entrance, and therefore, were not accorded any special status." Marcus turned again to the Indian woman, who undoubtedly was a leader, and said, "Aloosi harras eitlli sliit llit e sitnll?" As he spoke, he brought his right hand to the level of his right hip.

The woman spoke with some tribesmen to her left, and then spoke at length with the Professor. The language was like nothing Dov or Mariah, let alone Andrew had ever heard, and they could understand virtually nothing of what was being said.

Marcus turned again toward Dov, Mariah, and Andrew. The journalist had been taking notes of their encounter in a small notepad he had retrieved from his pocket. Marcus was clearly excited about what he'd learned. "They know where Jacob is, and they say he's safe."

"Will they bring us to him?" Mariah asked, with relief.

"They don't have to, because the boy and your friends, Dov, are making their way towards us."

"Well, I for one don't want to wait." Mariah snapped. She looked at the Indian woman. "Which way do we go to meet them?"

The Indian woman looked blankly at Mariah, and then turned to the Professor for a translation.

"Eetra tilwiidnl iql; tislin wliidisli mc i.wezoiii," he said hesitantly.

The Indian woman spoke, and two young men, with quivered arrows, leapt to the Professor's side. The men led them down a new passage, this one lacking any artificial light and which was difficult to traverse due to its regular intersection with fast moving, subterranean streams. The floor of the passage was occasionally covered with up to half a foot of guano, a fact Dov found intriguing and Mariah revolting.

They often had to wait for Andrew to catch up, for he insisted upon taking the time to stop so he could map their route in his notepad. Impatient, Mariah voiced her belief that the mapping stops were merely a ruse for the fat journalist to rest, but Andrew insisted that if they got separated from their guides, his map would become invaluable to finding their way back to their Indian hosts.

They soon heard the sound of a waterfall, and its noise became almost deafening as they approached it from its crest.

"Mom. Mom."

Mariah searched the passage for some sign of Jacob, but saw nothing.

"Here." Out of the gloom at the other edge of the waterfall's crest were a group of Indian warriors, and bursting from their midst was Jacob, who tried to ford the turbulent stream leading over the waterfall. The Indians pulled him back and apparently chastised him in Anasazi.

The Professor rushed forward, only then recognizing that Darstow and Colonel Hess were part of the party accompanying Jacob. "Are you all right, son?" Marcus asked.

"Hi, grandpa," the boy said, still a bit flustered at nearly being swept up by the swift current.

Marcus spoke to the Indian guide to his right. "Itos oi slkm sliekdk alie smlck siidmcxqa."

The man jogged to a narrowed part of the stream, where he forded it. The Indian used his long bow as a cane, steadied himself and gauged the water's depth at being shoulder high. Upon reaching the other side, he spoke with his fellow tribesmen, the tallest of whom placed Jacob on his shoulders and then attempted to ford the stream.

It was at that precise moment that dawn broke. With it returned the millions of bats that had exited the cave at dusk for their nightly meal.

CHAPTER SEVENTY-TWO

Leonard Island, New Mexico

One by one, as they entered the cave, the bats unconsciously switched off their radar, for they had memorized the route to their roosts. As the dawn brightened, what had started as a trickle of bats entering the cave had become a flood.

Just as Jacob and his Indian porter were in midstream, the flood of blind bats crashed into them and toppled Jacob into the fast moving water. The bats crashed into everyone at the crest of the waterfall.

Mariah screamed in terror. "Jacob," she cried, as she jumped into the turgid stream.

But she was far too late. As soon as the bats made their appearance, Darstow had wrestled away from Thomas's grasp, plunged into the water, and managed to snatch the boy by his back collar despite the agent's bound hands.

Dov had followed Mariah into the stream, as had Thomas, and all were hurtling toward the crest of the waterfall, which appeared to drop at least 100 feet onto a reef of sharp rocks and jagged boulders.

Marshaling his reserve of strength, Darstow managed to drag himself and the boy onto a shallow reef at the edge of the waterfall. As Dov, Mariah, and Thomas swept towards him, he shouted, "Back off, or I'll take the boy with me over the fall." As he spoke, he swung Jacob over the edge.

The pursuers backed away as best they could in the swift current.

"What do you want Darstow?" Marcus yelled.

"Same as before, Professor," Darstow replied. "You let me have the spaceship, and I'll give you the boy."

"And how do you propose to make that happen?" Marcus asked.

Darstow thought a moment. He turned to Old Vic and Dr. Anthony. "Well now, first thing is, you folks be kind enough to untie Colonel Hess over there, and give him one of those submachine guns. And then the rest of you can drop your weapons, and lead me to the spaceship. And as soon as you do, Colonel Hess and I will let you all go."

"And how long will it be, Keenan, before you come searching for me to figure out how to operate the ship?" Marcus inched his way towards Darstow's position.

Darstow renewed his grip on Jacob. "You really are not as important as I initially thought, Marcus," he replied. "With new computer modeling, we'll have the ship open and operating within two weeks. But I'd rather die than let you fly away forever in that thing, and so if I'm going to die, at least I'll die with the satisfaction of knowing I took your grandson with me." He glared at Marcus malevolently.

"All right, you win," the Professor sighed. He looked at Dr. Anthony. "Please untie the Colonel, and give him your weapon."

After Thomas nodded his assent, Anthony complied with the Professor's instructions. Marcus instructed the Indian warriors to disarm as well, although they did so with extreme reluctance.

After Hess shouldered his submachine gun, Darstow slowly inched back into the current toward Marcus Aaron, careful not to lose his grip on Jacob, who was hyperventilating from the icy water.

Just as Darstow appeared to gain a footing on the far bank, he slipped into a deep hole, sinking over his head and temporarily losing his grip on the boy. Mariah lunged toward Jacob, and managed to grab him by the belt. When Darstow resurfaced, he struggled towards the boy and Mariah, who had been swept toward the edge of the falls. All three washed up onto the narrow reef at the falls' crest, and it was there that the two adults began fighting over the boy.

"Shoot her, damn it!" Darstow cursed.

Without hesitation, Hess flipped his Uzi from auto to single fire mode.

"Amazing grace, how sweet the sound." Marcus sang.

Hess lowered his gun, perplexed by the Professor's burst of song.

"That saves a wretch like me." the Professor continued, off key. He pleaded, "Sing, Mariah, sing."

Mariah glanced at her father, perplexed.

"I once, was lost, but now I'm found," Dov and Andrew joined in. They looked at Mariah expectantly.

Hess did not want to shoot the defenseless woman. He brought the Uzi to his shoulder, and took careful aim at Mariah's upper left shoulder. The woman continued to struggle with Darstow over the boy.

It was only when Hess's sights were on her that Mariah remembered her father's instructions about the repelling belt. She gasped for air and desperately joined the chorus of *Amazing Grace*. She was unsure of the words after the first verse, and stumbled over the lyrics.

Mariah's singing caused Hess to further hesitate, but his resolve to shoot hardened after Darstow screamed, "Shoot her, you idiot!"

Hess fired. At that range, the Colonel could not have missed, but miraculously, due to Mariah's repelling belt, the round ricocheted into Darstow's chest, which blossomed into a crimson rose.

Darstow released his grip on Jacob and looked at Hess in astonishment. Without a word, he fell backwards into the rushing falls.

Hess watched in disbelief as his superior disappeared over the crest of the raging torrent. He turned to Thomas, who stood in waist deep water alongside the near bank. "I couldn't have missed." Hess exclaimed.

Thomas looked at Hess in disgust. "Let's end this, Colonel. Haven't enough people been killed today?"

As Hess stood frozen in indecision, Dov struggled over to Mariah and Jacob, and led them towards the far bank where the Professor stood. Mother and son shook from hypothermia, and Dov tried to warm them with his body. As he did so, he turned to Hess, his voice shaking from the cold. "Colonel, I am now your superior. Drop your weapon, and give us a hand."

Broken, Hess slowly nodded his head and complied. He crossed the stream with Old Vic, Dr. Anthony, and the remaining Anasazi warriors, and together, they headed back up the passage towards the docking bay leading to the shuttle.

CHAPTER SEVENTY-THREE

Leonard Island, New Mexico

"What will happen to them?" Mariah nodded to the crowd of Anasazi ringing the hatch to the shuttle, where the Professor, Mariah, and the rest had gathered.

Dov paused, unsure of the answer. "I don't know. My report of what happened here will certainly be classified, and so, barring the folks who believe Mr. Sawyer's dispatches, the only people who will know of the Anasazi will be high-ranking government personnel. Of course, we'll closely study all of the electronics in this room. But I'll try to make sure that the rights of these people are respected. That is, if I still have a job after I make my report."

Mariah looked at Dov squarely. "You know, if you lose your job, I bet you could find work in Santa Fe."

Dov smiled. "You mean I wouldn't ruin the neighborhood?"

Mariah kissed him on the cheek and held him close. "Any man who would sacrifice his job, put his very life on the line, all to simply do the right thing, can ruin my neighborhood any time."

Dov's heart nearly burst.

Marcus turned to Mariah. Jacob clung to her side, unwilling to release her for even a moment. "Ladies and gentlemen, it's time we left."

Marcus, Dov, Mariah, and Jacob crowded into the shuttle, leaving Thomas, Andrew, Old Vic, and Dr. Anthony, along with Colonel Hess and the remnants of his assault team, behind.

"Will I see you again old friend?" Thomas asked Dov.

Dov thought a moment. "If not, I want you to know you're my favorite goyim."

"And you're my favorite mensch."

And with that, the shuttle hatch silently slid shut.

CHAPTER SEVENTY-FOUR

Low Earth Orbit

It was several hours before Dov came to grips with the fact that he was in space, high above his planet, in an alien spaceship, which in a few hours, would hurtle to a planet called Deminia, quite possibly never to return to Earth again. He couldn't stop staring out the large viewing window at the eternal reach of space, and the resonating glow of the surrounding carpet of stars that pierced through the night with an intensity he could never have imagined.

They had spent several hours touring the ship, the Professor describing endless wonders, most of which Dov was unable to remember. Damn, if all he could think about was one thing–would Mariah go to Deminia with her father, or return to Earth with him?

He was glad to see that Dr. Pentov had met up with the Professor, and that Brittany Bourassa had come to no harm. He found Mariah's children delightful, and he was consumed with the foolish notion that he would marry Mariah and they would all live happily ever after in Santa Fe.

But hadn't he betrayed his country? America would undoubtedly benefit from reverse engineering the shuttle and ship, and wasn't he compromising national security in not securing both vehicles for his government?

"We will return someday."

Dov turned to find the Professor behind him.

"What do you mean?"

"You could have captured me, and held me and my family hostage to wring the secrets out of the shuttle, and perhaps the ship. Instead, you let us go. And that, Agent Bar-Lev, means a lot."

Dov looked confused.

"It means you value my freedom more than anything– a quality the Deminians would admire. And I suspect that a person who holds such values dear would be someone with whom the Deminians would like to visit."

"I would like to meet them," Dov said.

"And so perhaps you shall."

The Professor looked at his watch and then turned and walked to the main lobby where Mariah, Jacob, Brittany, and Trixie stood, all with anxious looks. "In less than twenty-four hours, this ship will be returning to Deminia, whether we like it or not. Trixie discovered that when she inadvertently communicated with my friend, Lthor, last night."

Marcus looked brave, but the realization that he was about to be leaving his daughter and grandchildren behind caused his eyes to well up with tears. He fought them back and pulled Trixie to his side. "Trixie and I will miss you all. We want you to know that wherever we are, we will be thinking of you always."

Jacob and Brittany ran to Marcus, and he hugged them. Mariah held her father as well, and rejoiced in his scent she always felt so calming.

After a few moments, Marcus pulled them away. "Dov, I expect you to see that they come to no harm."

"They will outlive you."

Marcus laughed. "Actually, since this ship travels at many times faster than the speed of light, I could travel to Deminia and return to Earth without aging significantly, although at the time of my return, you might be an octogenarian."

"Then return with an arthritis cure," Dov said. "I'm sure by then, I'll need one."

Marcus chuckled "I have programmed the shuttle to set you down at the lodge at Medicine Stone. You must exit quickly, because it will automatically begin its return journey back here within five minutes of landing."

Marcus walked to the opposite end of the lobby and touched a small button on the wall. Silently, the wall opened to reveal a recessed space that housed a small turquoise pendant with elaborate silver filigree surrounding its edges. Marcus pressed it into Mariah's hand.

"This pendant is a pager of sorts. It is only activated by your tears, or those of your children. If you cry onto the pendant, dear, really cry. I will know you need me, and I will do my best to return, assuming the Deminians can somehow cure my cancer."

"But, I don't want you to go in the first place."

"But go I must. And I can probably only return once, and almost certainly only in an emergency. So don't call me unless you really need me, like to walk you down the aisle at your wedding!" With that, Marcus winked mischievously at Dov and sealed the shuttle hatch.

" I hope we see him again," Dov whispered.

Mariah nodded, taking his hand in hers.

CHAPTER SEVENTY-FIVE

Leonard Island, New Mexico

A stranger convoy had never left Leonard Island. Agent Russo, Colonel Hess, and the remainder of the assault team led in the Blackhawk. They were followed by Old Vic, Dr. Anthony, and Thomas in the skiff, themselves followed closely by Boris and Waldo who, buoyed by their substantial blubber, had little trouble dog paddling furiously after their master, although it was clear they were not really comfortable in the deep water.

At times, Waldo and Boris got so close to the skiff their huge wakes nearly swamped the boat, and Thomas remarked to Old Vic, "It's a good thing we didn't take that damn recliner like you wanted; the extra weight would have sunk us for sure."

Vic laughed. "You shot that chair up on purpose, dint you?"

"It serves you right for all those years of force feeding me corn dogs and Strohs."

"Jacob seemed to like them just fine."

Thomas embraced Old Vic. "You'll miss him, I know."

"Hell, I will; he's com'n to work fer me next summer, taking care a the bears and painting an such."

"Maybe you ought to take him on an overnight to Tuzigoot, like your father did with you?"

After a while, the old man smiled. "Yer right. That boy and I just might uncover us some mysteries of our own."

Nothing further was said as the skiff slowly headed for home.

ISBN 141208577-2